KAHANA

THE HATHAWAYS BOOK 2

KATHI S. BARTON

This is a work of fiction. Names, characters, places, and incidents are products of the author's imagination or are used fictitiously and are not to be construed as real. Any resemblance to actual events, locations, organizations, or persons, living or dead, is entirely coincidental.

World Castle Publishing, LLC
Pensacola, Florida
Copyright © 2026 Kathi S. Barton
Hardback ISBN: 9798278398295
Paperback ISBN: 9798891265004
eBook ISBN: 9798891265011
First Edition World Castle Publishing, LLC, January 5, 2026
http://www.worldcastlepublishing.com

Cover: Cover Designs by Karen
Editor: Karen Fuller

Chapter 1

Penrod looked over the scene again before shaking his head. Kids with guns were always messy and deadly. Three dead today when a twelve-year-old found his mother's gun and had played deadman, some kind of game that was made up, he was sure, and shot and killed his brother and two sisters.

He had a feeling that the boy who had done the shooting meant to kill them, but figured, like most games, he'd be able to reset the game, and they'd be alive. While he didn't know that for sure, he'd been told that's what happened before, and he didn't have any reason not to believe it happened again. An entire family gone because their mother hadn't locked up her gun, but had left it in the bedside table in the event her ex-husband came around again.

"The medical examiner is here. He said that once he's finished, then we can move the bodies." He nodded. "Also, the mom is home now. She's in the kitchen with one of the female officers, wondering what had happened. She knows but is wondering how it had happened to her."

"I'll talk to her in a little bit. I have to sort out

the things that are in here. Where's the boy?" He said that he was taken to the hospital to be examined. "He wasn't hurt, was he? I didn't think to check when he came out of the house with the gun still in his hands."

"He's just fine. Wondering like the rest of us what happened. He said that they were playing a game, and it went off. Three times? I don't think so. He claimed that his sisters were arguing, and it was getting on his nerves. I think this was the plan all along, but that's just me." He didn't have an answer either way, so he left it be. "He has an officer with him and will be arrested as soon as he's given the okay that he's fine. What do you want to do about the woman? Her ex is around, too. Just a heads up."

"I'll talk to her as soon as the ME is gone. Make sure that everything is recorded so that there are no missteps with this one." The officer said he'd make sure that things went according to book. "Good. Once the ME is finished, make sure you get as much recorded as you can. I don't want this one to go off on the bad side because we missed something vital."

"I'll make sure we do it right." Nodding again, he stepped onto the porch to answer his cell phone. It was his brother Stamos.

"I know you're working, but I have a question for you." He said that he might not have an answer right now, because he was really busy. "Then I won't keep you. What do you know of the shooting on Maple? I'm headed there now."

"You won't get much." His brother worked for the newspaper and was their number one reporter, especially on homicides. "We've only just arrived, and the bodies are still here. You more than likely won't get past the line."

He knew that he could say things like that to his brother, and he'd not use it in his report. They had an understanding between the two of them. Penrod wouldn't give him anything on the record, and Stamos wouldn't use anything he said in his reports. It worked out well for the two of them, and that was why his brother was doing so well. He knew that he'd get the right answers even if he had to tell him he was wrong about his conclusions.

"Thanks. I'll show up anyway just to see if I can get anything you can use." He said that would be all right by him. Something else that Stamos did was that he didn't use his name to get himself out of sticky situations. Again, it had worked out well for the two of them. "Be careful there. I know things are tense when there is a shooting."

After promising that he would, the two of them hung up their connection. Not wanting to go back into the house just yet, he made his way around the side of the house toward the kitchen, where he knew the mother was. He had a few questions to ask her about the shooting as well. Namely, what did she think was going to happen when she left a gun in an unsecure place where her kids knew where it was.

"My babies are all gone." He didn't remark; his first thought was that she knew this might happen. But he'd been jaded about his job before when it turned out the parents were directly involved in whatever was going on. Today, to him, at least, felt no different. "What am I going to do now?"

He asked her questions about the gun and the kids. Yes, they knew it was in there, and no, she had not known that they played with it while she was gone. Apparently, this wasn't the first time that they'd gotten the gun out to play with it, and she knew about it. At least that was what she admitted when he tripped her up on questioning. She told them that it wasn't a toy and that they were to leave it alone. Fat lot of good that had done them when they made a habit of playing with the gun while she was out.

"They always put it back before I came home. I figured they knew that it would kill them." She didn't look all that upset, and he noted it in his notebook. He asked her why she didn't have a gun safe or at least a lock box with a key. "And if my ex-husband came around, what was I supposed to do? It would have taken me forever to get it out and use it on him. By then, he would have strangled us all in our sleep."

Penrod didn't bother commenting on her observation about him strangling them in their sleep. How would they know he was there—he didn't like people anymore and thought that it was beginning to show in his attitude towards his job. After questioning her for an hour, he had her taken to jail to have more questions put to her. Her son, a twelve-year-old, had been arrested and was going to be tried as an adult. The mother would more than likely be arrested as well for the murders of her three children. She would if he had anything to do with it.

Heading back to his office when the mother was taken downtown, he filled out his report and did his job. It was getting to the point where he could do his job in his sleep. It wasn't often that they had a homicide in town, but when it happened, as he was the only officer who worked the cases, it was usually a big one. He was the only one who went to court when it came to a trial as well. Keeping his notes in neat order, he was nearly finished for the day when Kahana called him.

"I'm on duty in the emergency room today. I wanted to tell you how sorry I am that you caught this case." He said that it was bad because there were children involved. "It always is. I'm sorry for the mother, too. I'm betting she ends up in jail with her son. She's not allowed in the room with him, and she's having a fit. Are you on your way home?"

"Not yet. I have some notes that I want to write up in the event that it goes to trial. I'm sure it will, so I'm getting everything written down so that I can remember when I have to." He asked him how he could forget. "That's true, but it might be months, even years, from now before it goes to trial, and I want to be able to remember what was said and done. I'm assuming that you have to write up something as well?"

"Yes, just to cover our asses." He knew that feeling and didn't envy his brother working on the bodies of the three children. "I'll talk to you when you get home. I'm on here for another twelve hours today, and then I can go home. You be careful driving home, little brother."

"Always." As he was putting his paperwork away, he made sure that the timeline of the events was correct. He didn't want some slick attorney getting him on something so little as a couple of minutes that he didn't document. After he was finished up, he watched as the mom was questioned about the shooting. Again, it occurred to him that she didn't seem all that upset about losing her three children, but perhaps she was just as jaded as he was anymore.

By the time he made it to his condo, he felt dirty and exhausted. Taking a long, hot shower, he didn't bother with putting anything on but got into his bed naked. Glad that he had someone come into his place and clean up for him, he knew that resting on clean sheets was something that he looked forward to. Tonight was no different. Falling asleep immediately, he didn't move for the rest of the night.

Eating some cereal and having a cup of tea, he was out the door half an hour earlier than usual. Once he was on the road, he was careful of the kids getting on the school bus this morning and was glad that they seemed to be enjoying themselves while waiting for school to begin. He remembered those mornings when he had nothing to worry about but whether or not he'd gotten his homework done. He always did, but he'd still worry.

There was a lot of buzz about the shooting at the office. He looked over the report on the kid who had spent the night behind bars and was pleased that he didn't seem to have had a good night. Cruel of him, he thought, but once he figured out what he'd done, he was going to be a good deal more sorry. At least he hoped so. The kid was going to be spending a lot of time behind bars, and he'd better get used to it.

Kahana called him twice. Once to tell him that the autopsy was starting for the three kids. Then later in the evening, to tell him that they were finished. A single gunshot to the head was the method of death for the three of them, and there were no drugs in their system. He didn't expect there to be, but it was good to know that he'd been right about it.

The rest of his evening was spent on filling out paperwork on the shooting. It seemed like there was an endless amount of paperwork that he needed to fill out, but he did each one of them with his notes nearby. The mother had been arrested as he thought she would and put in a cell far from her son. It was going to be a lengthy trial for the two of them, and he couldn't wait to get it over with. Three lives had been taken, and there was a lot to answer for.

Penrod was due at his brother's house that night, and he wasn't looking forward to it. They'd not ask him questions about the shooting, but they would tell him how sorry they were for it happening. As soon as he was in the door, he nearly went home. All his brothers were there with Mac, too. He loved Axel's wife as much as he did his brother. Debra Author was there as well, and he greeted her with the same hugs that he'd given the rest of them. She seemed to be as much a part of the family as Mac was, and he was happy.

"How's your heart acting up today?" Debra had had two minor strokes just two weeks ago that she was recovering from. If not for the quick thinking of Kahana, a doctor, she might well have died. The hospital was going to be sued when a nurse told Debra not to come in, wasting their time with indigestion again. "I hope you're doing what the doctor tells you. Kahana will make sure you're all right if you listen to him."

"I'm sticking to my cardiac diet as I've been told and getting my amount of stress under control as well. It's difficult with everything going on, but I'm working on it." He told her that he was proud of her. "I am as well. I never want to go through that again. It was scary."

Her grandda had died around the time she'd been having the symptoms of the heart trouble. Her cousin, Phil, as everyone was calling him because he hated the shortened version of his name, had brought a will to the reading of the will, and they allowed him to clean out the law office that Debra was to inherit. In addition to the hospital being sued, she was also suing the law firm that had allowed access to the firm by her cousin, and he'd been arrested as a result.

"We'll be eating soon. Your mom has made me something different than what you guys are eating, and that's about the sweetest thing I've ever had done for me." Penrod told her that her mom worried about her as well. "You've all been so good to me, and I feel loved. Now if only I can get the will taken care of and my firm up and running, I can get back to normal. Or whatever that word means to people nowadays."

"It doesn't mean all that much to me anymore. I

think normal is highly overrated." They both laughed, and she thanked him. "It's all right. I needed a good laugh, too. It's been a hell of a couple of days."

"I bet it has." She didn't ask, but he could tell that she wanted to. Being an attorney, she'd know better than most not to talk about an ongoing investigation. When she sat down and did her breathing the way she'd been told — in her nose and out her mouth, he sat quietly beside her. She would stress out easily, but she seemed to be getting a handle on things better daily. "I don't want to get overwhelmed by the stress that I'm having. I have to learn to control what I can. I'm trying, but it's difficult to do sometimes."

"You do what you need to do, and the rest of us will be here for you when you need it. There isn't any problem that big that you'll have to take it on by yourself. Just breathe, and you'll be fine." Debra nodded and told him it was getting easier. "I hope so. You need to take care of yourself over anyone else that's around."

They talked about the weather and how the storm had knocked a few trees down. It was safe topics, and she seemed to be all right with them. He even told her about his morning at home, getting ready for work when he'd nearly left the house with two different kinds of shoes on. He'd had to go back in his place twice because he'd forgotten his keys, too.

She laughed at his mistakes, for which he had intended, and they enjoyed their visit. When dinner was called, he walked with her to the dining room table and even pushed her chair in for her. Kahana sat beside her on the other side when he sat down. He wondered if Kahana had a thing for the pretty attorney and was going to try to get him to admit it by asking Debra out. She said yes, and he could see the steam coming off the top of his brother's head when he heard about it. Good. Maybe he'd get his butt in gear.

~*~

Kahana wanted to pop his brother in the head when he asked Debra out. He didn't know why; he didn't want to date her. But the thought of his brother getting to her first irked him something terrible. He decided to ignore her and his brothers for the rest of the night.

"Do you have rounds in the morning?" He glared at his brother. "Don't look at me like that. You've had every opportunity to ask her out, and you didn't. Next time, be a man and ask the woman out."

"I don't know why I'm so pissed at you." Penrod nodded as if he understood. "What? You know that I was going to ask her out, or you thought that I was."

"Frankly, I don't care. She said yes to me, and I'm going to take her to dinner. She's a nice, very attractive woman, and I've not been out on a date in more weeks than I can remember. You want to date, then find yourself someone else." He growled at Penrod. "Oh, come on. You know that's not going to bother me. I'm the one who carries a gun all the time. You'll have to be meaner if you want me to be afraid of you." He stretched his neck twice and heard it finally pop.

"You always have the best luck with women." He said because he was cute. "Nah, you're ugly as sin, and you know it. The only reason she said yes is because she felt sorry for you. That's it, isn't it? You told her how you can't get a date because of your ugly puss, and she felt sorry for you."

"You're just jealous. And have you looked in the mirror of late? Christ, it's small wonder you don't scare little children when you're out. Speaking of which, are you on rounds in the morning? I might need your help." He asked him what he needed because he could always change his schedule around. "I have a big table that's finally finished from the jackasses Spindle and Son. I was wondering if you could help me finally get it into storage. I was going to put it into a house, but I've never gotten around to looking for one. I'm sick of condo life."

"I am as well. Every time I come here to Axel's home or the parents, I realize what I'm missing in being between people who have no tolerance for noise. And all I'm doing is walking across the floor to the kitchen. Or they hate it when I take a shower when I get home from work. I know it's late, but damn, do they have to pound on the walls every time?" Kahana said he understood. Sometimes he takes two showers a day, and they get pissy with him. "We need to find ourselves a place that has our own four walls and no neighbors."

"I'm all for that." Kahana looked at Debra. "You take her out and then no more. I have no idea why I feel like knocking the shit out of you for asking, but don't do it again. All right?"

"Yeah, sure. But you might want to clear that with the others, too. I'm thinking that she's going to be busy for the next several weekends by the way that Audon and Stamos are eyeing her." He could see it then, his brothers vying for her attention. He didn't know how to make his intentions known without pounding a few heads. Instead, he let them have their fun. He was going to get his turn soon, and that would be the end of it. He looked over at Penrod when he said his name. "You're looking murderous. Please tell me that you're not going to pick a fight with them in here? If you do, then Axel is going to murder you. He just got his house all set up."

"I'm fine. Really, I am. I don't know why it bothers me so much, but it does, and there is nothing I can do about it, so I might as well give it up." He looked at Penrod then. "You're a good brother, and she'd be lucky if you found a wife in her."

"Let's not go that far. It's only a date. And to be honest, I only asked her out so that I could see your reaction." He rolled his eyes. "Well, it got you thinking, didn't it? Christ, the look on your face was priceless. If I had known I'd have gotten that kind of reaction from you, I wouldn't have done it at all. I'm sorry."

"Axel has spent the most time with her. I've only talked to her a few times, but we seem to be all right. She accuses me of having a terrible bedside manner, and I tease her. I worry about her heart all the time. She's lucky that I went with them when they went to her house to close it up. To think that one of the staff had told her not to waste their time by coming in bothers me on so many levels." He said it would him as well, and he'd not been there when she had her first heart attack. "It wasn't as bad as it could have been. Knowing the signs is what saved her life. Then getting her to the hospital when we did that was the real lifesaver for her. She's doing well now, making sure she's eating right and doing her breathing. She was under a great deal of stress. I don't know that she's not still, but she seems to be handling it better than before. I think it scared her as well."

"Sure it did. I know it would have me as well." Penrod smiled at him. "You got it bad, big brother. I'd ask her out now if you want to be able to do it this summer."

"I think that I will." He got up and sat back down. "If I asked her out, what will you think of me poaching on your woman?" They both laughed, and Kahana felt better about asking.

He really didn't want to step on anyone's toes, but the need to take her out on a date seemed imperative to him. Kahana wondered if his brother Axel had felt the same way when he met Mac. They fell in love so quickly, yet it seemed like they'd been together forever.

He got up to find Debra and found her in the kitchen with his mom and Mac. They all three stared at him like he didn't belong there, and he nearly left them to whatever they were doing. He started to back away when his mom called him in. Going into the kitchen with the women, he nodded at Debra after getting a hug from his mom.

"We were just discussing Debra and her heart issues. She was wondering if she was in the wrong profession to be having heart issues." He immediately went into doctor mode and told her of her stress levels and what she had to do to make sure she didn't have any. Commenting on her eating habits, as well as her going all day on very little to drink, wouldn't help her at all if she were trying to relieve some of her stress.

"See? I told you that he'd know you could do it. So long as you're careful. You've been given a chance, and you don't want to mess that up by having another heart attack when there isn't anyone around to save you. You were so very lucky this time."

"I was. And I still am." He told her that he'd be there for her whenever she had any questions. "All right. What are you doing next Friday night? I have this ball for the local attorneys to go to, and I need someone to go with me to keep me calm." He told her how he'd come in to ask her if she was busy anyway. "Then good. If you don't mind that we go out in black tie, then you can be my date."

"I'd love it. And you don't need me to keep you calm, Debra. You're doing a good job of that all on your own. So long as you remember what you've been taught, you'll be fine." She said that she didn't feel fine when her breathing got out of control. "Just breathe, and if you have to, find a nice quiet place to sit. Don't overthink things, and you should be fine."

"But you'll still go with me, right? I mean, since you know that I can do this, you'll still go with me, right?" He said it would be his pleasure. "Good. I need you there. I could have asked Penrod, who asked me out for this weekend, but I want you there for some reason. Maybe because you're a doctor, I don't know. But I'm glad that you'll be there."

He didn't like to think that he was going only because she might need him as her doctor, but he was going to take what he could get. At least she didn't ask one of the others to take her, and he was happy with that. As soon as the kitchen was cleaned up, Mom and Mac left them in the kitchen. He had so much to say to her that he didn't know where to begin.

"I came to find you to ask you out." She told him she was sorry that she'd asked first. "I'm not. I'm glad you did. I would have fumbled it all up, and my mom would think she raised an idiot. And don't get me started on what Mac would say. She'd cut me no slack at all."

"She is a bit intense." He thought that was an understatement but didn't comment. Debra sat down on one of the many stools that were around the breakfast bar in the kitchen. "Do you really think that I'm going to be all right? I don't mean just at the ball thing that I'm required to go to. I mean, in general, am I going to be all right?"

"You're young and healthy, always two things that help out in any illness. But you're not giving up because you've had two heart attacks. Some people would. If you take care of yourself and make sure that you're doing what we tell you, you'll live another seventy or more years." He sat down when she offered him a place beside her. "Worrying won't help either.

You have enough stress as it is without adding to it. This thing with Phil? You should just let Axel handle it for you. He's good at what he does, as I'm sure you are. And if it gets to be too much, tell him. He'll know enough to stop where he is and help you out."

"I don't want to be pampered all my life, but I feel like that's what I'm doing to myself." He shook his head and told her that she was getting used to something new. "That's true. I find myself reading labels on things before I put them into my cart."

"Good. More people should do that, too." They talked about the ball a little bit, and he was glad that he'd asked her what sort of tie it really was. She told him how she was wearing a formal gown and that if he had one, a tux would be great. "I just so happen to have one. Mom had us all buy one when we started going out more. She said you'd never know when you had a need for one, and she's right. But then she usually is."

"I like your family. They get along so well. I've never gotten along with mine. My grandda only left me the firm because I was the only one who was an attorney. He didn't care all that much that I was a woman, too. I'm hoping that Axel can get Phil to return all the things that he stole from me in a timely manner. I have no place to live as of tomorrow. Nor do I have a job to go to." He told her that there was a condo in his area that was open. "I have nothing to put in it. I'm about as broke as I've ever been in college with student loans out the ass."

"I can help you out. And don't say no until you hear me out. Axel is going to be able to get everything back for you, and you can pay me back then. Axel is that good." She said she really didn't know how long that was going to be. "I'm fine with helping you. In fact, it would be my pleasure to help you out. I feel like a knight in shining armor right now."

They talked about what she would need, and he told her that he had a spare bed that he wasn't using, as he was looking for a house too. She told him that she'd had her heart set on a house as well, but with all this going on with Phil, she didn't know how long that was going to take either. Things were up in the air until she could get the money and the firm back from Phil.

"He's always been a person who messed things up. If things were perfectly laid out and he agreed with them, he'd find some way to mess it up so that it's all fucked. He's been like that my entire life." She did her breathing again, and he took her hand into his. "That's nice. I needed that. Thank you."

"Again, it's my pleasure. You're very easy to talk to. And I'm glad that I got to know you. How about I take you over to the condo now, and you can have a look around? It's right on the way to your home, where you're staying." She told him that she only had one more night in the place before they were going to come in and clean it up for the next person. "That's fast. I guess there is a lot of that going around. Housing is so short around here."

"I know. I've been trying to find a small rental until things are taken care of, and that's not going to happen. I do want to see the condo if you have time. I could surely use some good news." They got up to leave, and Penrod gave him a thumbs-up. Kahana did feel good about taking her home.

Chapter 2

Debra thought that the condo was too small, but she was going to take it. It was the first thing that she'd been able to look at since she'd been searching. With the little bit of furniture that she was going to get, just a bed and a dresser, she would be fine for the next several months until Axel got her things squared away with her Grandfathers estate.

"I'm going to bring over the spare bed in my other bedroom for you to use. It's a queen, but big enough for you to start out with." She said she'd take it. "Good. There's a dresser that goes with it that my brothers are going to come over and help me move. Mom has some dishes and such, you can have too, that she was going to donate to the local Goodwill."

"This is what I mean when I said you guys are the best." He said they were just helping out a friend. "A friend that you barely know. I appreciate it more than you can understand. I thought that I was going to be living out of a box by this time tomorrow."

"We'd never let that happen to you. Even if we barely know you, you're still a good friend. And someone that we all like." She wanted to be held by Kahana, but there was a knock at the front door. "That'll be my family. They said they'd be right over, and I guess they weren't kidding."

The place was much smaller feeling with them all in it. Once Kahana and two of his brothers went next door to his place, they were taking the bed apart, and it didn't feel much better. It wasn't until Katie, Kahana's mom, took her into the kitchen area that she felt better. Smiling at the woman for understanding, she looked at the box of dishes that she'd brought to her.

"I got them on sale once, thinking that I'd change out our everyday stuff. But it's only a four-place setting set, so that wouldn't work. I have a few pots and pans for you, as well as a box of silverware that has been just sitting around the house for years. It's still good, but again, I never got around to changing it out."

By the time they all left around midnight, she was exhausted. However, she had everything she needed to live on her own for the next several months. Axel assured her that it wouldn't be that long—with the exception of food. And since she now had a place to live, getting food wouldn't have been as daunting as it might have been less than twenty-four hours ago. She was going to pay it forward as they told her to do as soon as she could. Good people were hard to find nowadays, and she thought that she'd found the best of the best in the Hathaways.

When Kahana left a little after one, she made her way to the bedroom. The bed was a perfect fit in the room, and she was going to bring her clothing over tomorrow to put them away in the nice big dresser. Things were looking up for her, and she was so happy. Getting into the nice, clean bed, she thought of all the things that she was going to do to pay back the Hathaways. First and foremost, she was going to thank them for the rest of her life. She owed them everything.

Getting up the next morning, she felt better than she had in months. She was refreshed and feeling like a new person. After her shower, she decided to treat herself to something to eat out and then get herself some food. She wouldn't know how she could have done it without help. Just as she was going out the door, Kahana was there with coffee and muffins. He said that he'd gotten her a mixed berry and himself a chocolate chip. She was suddenly starving to death.

After eating with him, she felt like she was too full to shop, and thought it was a good time to shop, so she didn't overshop. She might have a place to call her own, but she was just one person and didn't eat all that much. Kahana offered to drive her as he had some things that he needed to pick up as well. She was glad for the company and told him so.

The two of them did a good job of not overspending. She really did read the labels and was glad that he was there to answer questions about some of the ingredients that were in the food she was getting. He told her fresh was the best, and she took him up on that. Buying what she needed in the produce area had her cart full of things that she loved and would be good for her.

After getting things put away when they were finished, she went to talk to Axel about the things that were going on with Phil. He was still in jail, and it looked like he was going to be there for a while. She was glad for it. Having him lurking around all the time scared her. He wasn't a nice person.

Axel told her what he'd been able to find out. The firm in charge of reading the will was being sued by her as well, and they wanted to settle. She thought it was a good idea, but Axel warned her that there might be more money if she were to wait until it went to trial. Agreeing with him, he said that he'd get back with them as soon as tomorrow. The settlement wasn't nearly what she thought it should be, and she was glad that he'd suggested she wait. They had done her wrong, and they were going to have to pay for it.

After getting her signature on some paperwork, the two of them talked about what she should expect next. It was all things that she knew were going to happen, but she was glad for Axel's input. He had more experience than she did about this sort of thing, and she was glad that he was on her side. She'd never win if he were on the other side of the table from her; she just knew it.

Going back to her home, she decided to take a nap. She'd been doing that a great deal since she'd gotten out of the hospital, and she felt better when she got up. Lying down on the bed, her mind seemed to be centered on Kahana, and she had to smile. She wondered what he would think if he knew that he was the first person she thought of in the morning and the last person she thought of when she went to bed. Her naps were no different in that she thought of him all the time.

When she woke up, she checked her phone and saw that she had one missed call. Since it was Kahana, she listened to the voicemail and decided that having dinner with him tonight sounded good. Calling him back, she got his own voicemail and left a message telling him she'd love to have dinner with him tonight. Not ten seconds after she closed the connection, he called her back.

"I'm working on something at work and might be able to get off earlier than I planned. How does pizza and cola sound? You can treat yourself to that once in a while, but don't make a habit of it." She told him that it sounded good. "Good. I'll pick you up at four unless something else comes up. It's been a pretty slow day, but I'll call you if things pick up. Are you resting like you should be?"

"I was taking a nap when you called me." He told her that she needed to do that all the time. When she was tired, she needed to just go to sleep. It was the best medicine for her. "I agree. I feel so much better when I get up. Like I've been given a new outlook on life."

"Good for you." After hanging up with him, she took a shower. She'd had one this morning, but she wanted to be fresh when they had their date. She had a date with Penrod tomorrow night and wasn't looking forward as much as she had been. Hanging out with Kahana had been the highlight of her week, and she didn't know what to do about her upcoming date with his brother.

Kahana called her at two to tell her that he was going to be later than he thought, but no later than six. She was fine with that as she'd eaten an apple to tide her over and was doing well. As soon as he pulled into the parking lot, the two of them kissed, and it was perfect. Once she was in his car and they were on their way, all she could think about was how much she'd enjoyed it. It wasn't as if she'd never been kissed before, but this one was special. It was their first of many, she hoped.

Dinner was fun, and she was careful to eat a salad before the pizza arrived. It tasted really salty to her, and she couldn't believe it after it had only been a couple of weeks since she'd cut salt out of her diet. But she enjoyed the meal and the company, and that was the best part of it all. She was beginning to fall for the man, and she wondered what he'd do if he found out. More than likely, drop her like she was something out of a nightmare.

"There are two different places that I want to take you the next time we have dinner. One of them being seafood. Do you like it? It's good for you, too." She said that she loved seafood as it was one of her favorite meals. "Good. It's one of my favorites as well. The other place is a steakhouse that serves chicken as well. I don't know how you feel about red meat, but you shouldn't eat too much of it."

"I don't anyway. I do like chicken that is grilled, but not fried. All that extra fat I know isn't good for me, so I've been avoiding it since I got out of college." She was happy when he took her hand from across the table. "You and I are beginning a relationship here. I'm not upset or sad about it, but I'd like to know what happens when I go out with your brother tomorrow night. I don't want any ill feelings going on between the two of you."

"I've spoken to Penrod about it. He said that he'd be on his best behavior. I'm not sure what that means, but I did tell him that you were beginning to mean something to me and that I wasn't sure that dating him was going to be all right." She said she could cancel. "No, don't do that. I think he's looking forward to it too much. But I'd like to ask you if, like me, you don't date anyone else. I've fallen for you in a big way, and I don't want to share."

"I feel the same way." The two of them finished their meal and were headed out before seven o'clock. By the time she got home, she was tired again and decided to tell Kahana that she was all for going to bed early.

She wasn't as weak as she'd been just two weeks ago; her strength was getting better daily, but she did tire and didn't want to get herself into something that would cause her to have another attack. That was why she was so glad that she was dating Kahana. He was forever asking her about her healthy habits, and she liked him for that.

Getting ready for bed, she did feel like she was sleeping a great deal; she turned off her phone and the alarm so that she could sleep through the night. If anyone wanted to get in touch with her, they could leave a message. She was too exhausted to bother with anyone tonight and was glad for the new place she was living. It afforded her a place to rest when she needed it without any stress.

She realized that she had not had to breathe

through any kind of stress today. Good, she thought to herself, perhaps she was getting better at handling it. Pulling the blankets up and over her shoulders, she laid there thinking about the kisses that they'd shared tonight and couldn't believe how much she was looking forward to seeing Kahana again. Rolling to her side, she closed her eyes and decided that if she kept this up, her feelings about him, she'd be in love with him in no time. If she wasn't about there already.

Closing her eyes, she felt herself drifting off and still thought about Kahana. She didn't know much about him, but the more time she spent with him, the more she fell in love with him. She did wonder what he'd say if she told him that. Would he tell her that he was falling for her too, or would he really run off and tell her to get a life? With a small giggle, she let her mind shut down while she slept. It was a good night for being inside, she thought. The rain was coming down hard.

Waking in the middle of the night to go to the bathroom, she could hear the shower in the condo next to hers. She had to think about where Kahana lived and knew that it was him. She wondered why he was up so late when he said he needed to get into bed too, as he had rounds in the morning, and frowned. Whatever was going on, she hoped he'd be all right for the rest of the day.

Sleep took her under again when she closed her eyes. The rain had stopped at some point in the early hours of the morning, and she was glad. Rainy days would make the emergency room busy because of slick roads, and she didn't want anyone, especially Kahana, overworked.

~*~

Kahana was in a terrible mood and knew he was taking it out on those around him. Twice he'd had to take several deep breaths before his mouth got the better of him, and once he'd had to leave the room or tell his patient off. He kept thinking about Penrod taking his girl out.

Not that they'd made any kind of commitment. She did tell him that she wasn't going to date anyone else while they were seeing each other, and he'd told her the same thing. But he couldn't help but think that Penrod wasn't going to be as nice as he was to her, and that bothered him. Penrod was about the nicest person he knew. But he was taking Debra out, and he wanted it not to happen.

"Doctor Hathaway? You have a phone call on line four. I think it's your brother, but he didn't say. He also said if you were busy, you could call him back." He went to the phone and pressed four to pick up the call. It was Penrod, and he felt his temper get the better of him. If not for his laughter, he might well have made an ass of himself in front of the staff. Instead, he waited for him to speak.

"I've just gotten off the phone with your girl." He asked what that was about, not even denying that she was indeed his girl. "We've canceled our date for tonight. She told me that she didn't think it was right with the feelings that she was having for you. I was going to call her anyway, but this way I'm not going to look like an ass and cancel on her myself." All his anger in that moment was gone.

"I'm glad. I wanted to suggest it myself, but you did ask her first, and that's the way it should have been." He thought about what his brother said. "What do you mean when she said that she was having feelings for me? Did she say what they were?"

"No, only that you and she have been seeing each other a great deal and that she felt it was wrong for her to go out with me when she knew nothing was going to come of it." He didn't say anything to his brother, but he was about as happy as he'd ever been. "You still there?"

"Yes. I was thinking of my feelings for her. They're big too." He felt his face heat up when one of the nurses giggled at him. "I'll talk to you later. I've some people that I have to apologize to that I've been snapping at all day. I'll be honest with you when I tell you it's been a rough day thinking about the two of you going out."

"Like I said, had she not called, I was going to cancel on her. I've seen the two of you out together and wondered if it was bothering you that I was taking her out. I shouldn't have done that. But it did have the desired effect. You realized that you like her." He said that he was falling in love with her. "I figured that much out on my own. All right, Kahana, I'll let you go and talk to you later. Since she had plans to go out anyway, where are the two of you going? You have to show her a good time."

All he could think about was her and the bed he'd lent her. Kahana wanted to make love to her in the worst sort of way and to stop taking cold showers in the middle of the night. He was going to have a hell of a water bill when the statement came this month, and he wasn't thrilled about paying it for cold, lonely showers.

For the rest of his day, things went smoothly. He did have some trouble with one of his patients wanting to leave the hospital, as they felt that they wanted to die at home. The person was nowhere near death, and he told them that. Still, he signed off on allowing them to leave as soon as possible to get home to their children. When he thought of Debra, heavy with his child, he nearly passed out in the hallway.

It had been a vision that was as clear as day

when he closed his eyes. Not only was she going to have a baby, but there was one on her hip as well. Holding onto the desk that was nearby, he wanted to go home right then and start on the process. Having her have his child was the most beautiful thing that he could have imagined. That was when it occurred to him that he loved her. Not just a little either; he was madly and completely in love with her.

He knew that for the rest of the day, he had a sappy smile on his face. One of the nurses commented on it, and he told her that he was thinking wonderful thoughts. She told him that he looked like he was in love and wanted to hug her. He wondered if anyone else could see how much in love he was with Debra and didn't care.

On his way home, he called Debra. She usually took her nap around this time, so he waited to talk to her when he got home. He didn't bother with knocking on her door for fear of waking her up, but went home and took another shower and changed. Whatever she wanted to do, he was up for it because he was a man in love. Doing a little jig, he got himself dressed as he was thinking of when would be the best time to tell her how he felt.

At just after six, she knocked on his door. He told her that he'd been waiting for her to take her nap, and she told him that she had just woken up. She told him about her broken date tonight, and he told her how his brother had already called him. She looked relieved to him, and he was glad for that as well.

"I've been thinking about you all day." He asked if he was in trouble. "No. Why would you be?" He told her he'd been thinking of her all day as well. "I've got some news for you, but I don't know how you're going to take it."

"I love you." She looked at him, surprised, and then she laughed. "I don't think that me professing that I love you is all that funny, my dear. What were you going to tell me?"

"That I've fallen in love with you as well. I know that it seems so soon, at least it does to me, but I can't think of anyone else but you at any given time of the day. It's like if I can't be with you, then I'm going to be thinking of you. Do I make any sense?" For an answer, he kissed her. "I guess that's a yes."

"It does. I've only just discovered how I feel about you today. When I was thinking about you going out with Penrod, I have to tell you it put me in a bad mood all morning. I've been telling people I'm sorry since it hit me that I was in love with you. One nurse said that I looked like I was in love to her, and all I could think about was telling her that I was. With you." She asked him what they were to do now. "I was thinking that we need a house to live in. A place that—

do you want children?"

"Yes. I would love to have children with you." He kissed her again. "You keep that up, and we'll never get things done around here. I would love to look at houses with you. I have one. Or will have one when your brother gets it back for me. I suppose I could ask the courts if I could go into it now, but I don't know what they'll say."

"Ask Axel and see what he has to say about it. Do you have an address?" She gave it to him as she was pulling out her cell to call his brother. He looked it up on the internet and saw that it was a huge house just the street over from his parents' home. Kahana read the facts on the house and was impressed that it had five bedrooms as well as five and a half bathrooms. It was a big formal house that he could see them living in.

"He said that he has the keys to it, and if we wanted to go see it, we could go tonight. Is that all right with you?" He told her that it was so long as she was all right with them living in it. "You mean if we see it, we might want it? I'm all for that. I know nothing about the house other than where it is and that it's furnished. I can't wait to see it."

Axel and Mac went with them to the new home. It was grander than he thought it was going to be, and knowing that all the furniture stayed with it made it seem all the more move-in ready for them. He particularly liked the home office, and the kitchen was up to date. The whole house was ready to be used, and he could see them living there for the rest of their lives. Axel pulled him aside when the two women went to look at the bedrooms.

"You and Debra planning on keeping house together?" He nodded with another sappy grin on his face. "Good. I think you two make a perfect couple, and you'll be a powerful one too. You a doctor and her an attorney? People will want to come to see you more and more as the weeks go by."

"What about the house? Can we move into it?" Axel said he'd look into it tomorrow with the other attorneys for the case. "Hopefully it's a different one than the one who had read the will that Phil provided."

"These people have been assigned the case when the other firm was arrested. They'll be fined too, just so you know. I think they want to get this off their books as much as I do, and they've been very good at keeping me informed. They have seized the money that Phil had taken, and this house was just one more asset that Debra was to get. Phil got nothing because of the many times that he had to be bailed out." He asked how much longer it could take. "I'm thinking not too much longer. Like I said, they want to get it finished with too, and now that the real will has been read, they'll be making sure that Debra and Phil get what's coming to them."

"By Phil getting what's coming to him, I'm assuming that it's nothing good." He nodded and said that was right. "Good. He doesn't deserve anything after the way that he's treated Debra. To think that the other firm took his word for it that he had the right will. What were they thinking about?"

"Who knows but it's all done now. Once he has his day in court, you can bet that he's going to be put back in jail for a long time. I hope for a few years, but I'm not working on that just yet. I'm filing claims against his estate, too, what little there is of it, but it will keep him from taking her money." He asked how much the estate was worth. "Billions. Billions upon billions. The old man knew how to invest, and he was a good attorney for all intents and purposes. It was a large firm that she's getting. With as many as a dozen partners."

"What would you do with it if it came to you?" he said that he'd give the other attorneys the opportunity to buy it from him and be done with it. "I'm guessing you don't want to own a large firm now that you're out on your own."

"I don't. The money would be great. But I'm not into babysitting a bunch of attorneys while they whine about their cases. That's all it was where I worked.

Men and women bitching about how much work they were doing without enough to pay for it. Some of those people that I worked with were partners and were making six figures off of each case. I love that I'm on my own and able to take the kind of cases that I want." Kahana whistled. "Tell me about it. I could have been that person if I had stayed a bit longer. I want nothing to do with big firms. However, if Debra goes the way I'm going to suggest to her, I'll take her on as a partner. We could work well together."

"I believe that she's been thinking about it too." He said that he'd mentioned it to her last week about selling the firm. "That's what she said. I don't know what she's going to do, but I'll support her in anything she desires to do."

"Good for you." As the two of them went over the bottom of the house, the girls were still upstairs. He knew that there were quite a few bedrooms in the place, but couldn't figure out what was taking them so long. He hoped that they were getting along. He wanted everyone to love Debra as much as he did. "We were going to catch something to eat if you want to join us. I know that she didn't have any plans. I think she called Mac to ask her about Penrod. I guess he took it well that she didn't want to go out with him."

"He told me that he was going to call her if she didn't call him. He was having second thoughts about it right after he asked her." Axel looked at the staircase when the two of them came down. "They look like they've been up to something. I wonder if it will bode well for the two of us. I like saying us. It's a great feeling to be in love with someone."

"I know." They ended up going to get dinner together, and while they were waiting for food, Axel made a couple of calls. The other firm decided that it would be one less thing they had to worry about if she would take the house off their books. All she had to do was come into the office and sign off on the paperwork, claiming that it was hers. "I'll go with you in the event there are any questions. All right?"

It was settled then. Axel would go in with Debra, and he'd be at work. Tomorrow night, they'd be able to stay in the big house, and it would be theirs. Debra had already said she was going to put his name on the deed as well as hers, and he was happy. They were homeowners. Mom and Dad would be pleased, too.

Chapter 3

Phil was pissed off. So far today, he'd had to see no less than four attorneys asking him questions about the real will and the fake one. He thought that it looked really good, at least good enough to have everything turned over to him in the first place. He loved it when a well laid plan came together. But now it had turned to shit.

Not only had this other firm seized his bank accounts, but they'd also voided his deed that said that his grandfather's house was his own. That hurt him the most. He loved that big place and could see himself living in it for the rest of his life. Of course, the furniture had to go. It was much like the old fat ass, old and ugly. But now even that wasn't going to be his dream. That damned Debra had ruined it all for him. Just because fat ass had liked her better.

He didn't know if he liked her better or not, but he certainly left her everything. Billions of dollars for his cousin rather than anything for him. He should have gotten it all and would have had it not for her sticking her nose into things. Had she just done what he'd told her to do and not show up at the reading, then he'd have everything his heart desired, including more money than he could spend in a lifetime. However, he was going to try to spend it all as fast as he could. The firm would be bringing in more money in addition to what he inherited.

He'd been told no less than ten times that he couldn't own the firm as he wasn't an attorney. Some stupid rule that he had plans on changing if he could, as soon as he was behind the big desk. And his grandfather had the biggest desk he'd ever seen. What difference did it make if he was a lawyer or not? Nothing that he could see. He wanted to reap the money that they made by taking a percentage of theirs. It was going to work out well in his favor, too, but for the law stating that he couldn't do it.

Then there was the insurance policy. That too had been worth millions of dollars, and he couldn't collect on it either. When his grandda had been sick with pneumonia last year, he'd taken out a policy on him to hedge his bets in getting some cash. When he tried to collect on it, they told him that he had not made any payments on it, so it was voided, too. Why would he have to make payments on a payout when the old man died? That was one of the stupider things that anyone had told him today. That and the fact that Debra was moving into the big house within the next couple of days.

That burned his ass, too. He'd wanted the big

place. It would have been grand for the parties that he'd planned on having. And Philipp had plans for some big parties too. He would supply the drugs, and everyone else would supply the food. He was counting on it being a weekly thing when he was in charge and was pissed off that it wasn't going to come to fruition. Just thinking about Debra would get his blood boiling.

"Mr. Author, you have a visitor." He asked if it was another attorney. "I don't believe so. I could ask, but then you'd not know until I took you back to your cell, as you only get one shot at visitors." He said he'd see them.

"But I'm not going to be happy if it's someone else telling me what I can't do. I have had enough of attorneys today." He bitched all the way up to the door and while being led to the room where he'd met the others. The woman who had been bitching about every little thing was seeing her lawyer, and she didn't seem all that happy about it. But he had a feeling that she was never happy about anything because she liked to be in charge. It was his cousin. "What do you want? Haven't you taken enough from me today? Every time someone comes to visit me, they have more shit for me to sign over to you. It's not fair if you ask me."

"I didn't, so that's fine too." She sat down when he was put in the chair. There were still chains on his hands so that he couldn't get to her, but he would if given the chance. He wanted to smack that smile right off her face. "I've come to offer you a deal."

"Are you giving up the will that was made out in your favor? That would be the only thing that I'd agree to." She stood up to leave, and he told her to tell him. "Why do you have to be such a pain in my ass for? What did I ever do to you to deserve such treatment?"

"You tried to take my inheritance for starters. Then there are the whole childhood beatings that you did to me when we were growing up. You always were a brat." Phillipp snorted and told her those were his fondest memories. "I just bet they were. Well, get over it. You're not going to touch me or what's mine again."

"Whatever helps you sleep at night, you go on telling yourself that." He asked her what the deal was. "And don't take all day in getting to the good part. I want to know how much you're going to give me of the estate that I should have inherited."

"I will give you one million dollars to move away from here and never bother me again." He said that wasn't enough. "That's more than you're going to get now, dumbass. Take it or leave it, there is no negotiating on my end."

"You're getting billions of dollars, and you're only offering me one million? That's not fair. Nor is it something that I'd entertain from you. You give me a billion, and I'll think about leaving town." She told

him no and stood up again. "You're going to stay right
here until I get more money from you. And don't think
I don't know what the estate is worth. You'll be making
a billion a year just after the firm gets its cut."

"I'm selling the firm." He asked her what
she'd said. "I said I'm selling the firm to the partners.
They've all agreed that they want it, and all they have
to do is come up with the amount that I want. And it's
nothing compared to what they'll be making once it's
a finished deal."

"Yet you still are only offering me a million
dollars. You're a bitch." She thanked him and told him
that the deal was on the table; did he want it or not?
"Not. I wouldn't take that much from you if it were
under threat of death. You should be happy that I'm
not asking for half of the estate."

"You won't get it either, so that's a moot point.
I'm leaving here, and you have twenty-four hours to
decide what you're going to do." He asked about jail
time. "I have nothing to do with that. You'll have to see
what happens when you get to court. I suppose I could
just wait and see how much prison time you get, then
you'd be away from me, but I was trying to make it so
that when you get out, whenever that might be, you
have something to fall back on."

"What makes you think I'm going to go to
prison?" Debra started listing the things that he'd done,

starting with the will that had been forged. "They don't care about that. I know that when I get out, I'm going to need more than just the pocket change that you're talking about. I'll have some real needs."

"Then I suggest that you take what I'm offering you and forget about me. It's the only way that you're going to survive. I'm getting married soon to a powerful family, and when I do, you won't be able to come near me with a ten-foot pole in your hands." He told her that he'd see about that. "Yes, we will. You just remember this while you're lying in your little cot at night, while there are hundreds of prisoners all around you. How you could have a million dollars waiting on you, and you turned it down."

"Damned right I'm turning it down." When she got up to leave this time, he let her. There was nothing more that could be said on the subject until she was willing to pay him what she owed him. And he didn't think that a billion dollars from her was going to hurt her at all. Hell, he'd spend a million dollars on his getting out of prison party he planned to have. If he made it to prison. And nothing was set in stone right now. He was going to get himself a good attorney and show her what it's like to be taken down by a cousin.

As he was being taken back to his cell, he thought of the money that he could get from Debra. She'd have so much of it that it would be hard for her to keep track of it all. He knew that he would be like his grandda said all the time, women weren't as smart as men. He knew that to be true, too.

Sitting in his cell, he listened to the old hag down from him. She was going on about her dinner and how they should give her what she wanted. She also bitched about her son and granddaughter too a great deal, and he was sick of hearing about them. He'd seen her have visitors, but it didn't seem to be anyone that she wanted to see, as she would scream at them to get away from her. Phillipp wondered who she was talking about and was glad that she wasn't related to him. He might well have to put her out of his misery someday if she harped on shit the way that she was doing all the time.

He had his own thoughts to occupy his mind, and it was the money that he was going to convince the courts to give him from the estate. It was the least they could do after Debra got it all. He would have one of the attorneys from the estate talk to Debra about him getting what he wanted. That was the ticket: get them to appeal to her sense of family.

Never bothering with Debra when they both became adults, he'd been surprised when she turned out so pretty. Grandda had always called her ugly, and he had gotten into the habit as well. He'd not noticed that she'd grown up into such a looker until he saw her at the reading of the will for his grandda. He wanted to smack her face right off her and be done with her when she brought herself an attorney who seemed to know his shit. Phillipp wondered if he was available to help him out of this jam and decided to figure out who he was. It couldn't hurt, could it?

For the rest of the evening, he thought about what he could do with a billion dollars. Debra would come around soon, he thought. She wasn't all that smart if she thought that he was going to just let this go. A billion dollars would go a long way in setting him up nicely. Now all he needed to do was get her to give it to him.

Dinner was served like it always was. They told you it was ready, and then they'd slide it across the floor to you. He heard the old hag bitching about that, too, and rolled his eyes. Phillipp had been in jail before, and one thing that you didn't do was mess with the officers bringing you your food. They'd spit in it or just happen to be out of things that you wanted. He had learned that the hard way. Apparently, the old hag hadn't learned anything by being in this jail.

The food wasn't that bad. There was plenty of it, too. Even the slices of cake or pie were bigger than you'd get in a nice restaurant. Tonight they were having chili dogs, and he got three of them. There was a nice pile of fries, too, that came with them, which had chili and cheese on top of them as well. He had soda to drink, two cans as well as a nice slice of lemony pie that was his favorite of all the desserts he'd been getting. He started on that first. No point in not having room for it at the end of the meal, he told himself.

After his dinner tray was taken away, he was asked if he wanted tea at the end of the night. It usually came with graham crackers or some cookies, always his favorite, so he told the cop that he was fine with that. If the old hag got anything extra, she no doubt bitched about it. The fact that she thought they should go to Columbus for her meals to him was funny. She even wanted a nice glass of wine to go with this meal. Like that was ever going to happen.

Lying down on his cot, he thought about the money again. He'd do something grand with that much money, then he'd spend it as fast as he could get it in his hands. To him, there was more where that came from, and he didn't care if he drained Debra dry before he was finished with her. She should have stayed out of his business, and she might be better off. He knew that he was going to be as soon as he got him an attorney who was worth his weight.

"I wish I'd of paid more attention to the man's name that got Debra what she wanted." He knew it was a long name. Even his first name should have been something that he could easily remember. But all he could think of was Asshole. He knew that wasn't right, but that's all that stuck in his head. "I'll get one of the half dozen attorneys that come here to tell me. That's what I'll do. And I'll have them contact him for a good payday too."

He didn't know how that was going to work without any money, but he could always talk a big game. Yes, sir, he told himself this was going to be just perfect for him, and he'd have all the estate money coming to him.

~*~

Debra enjoyed working on her own defense. Axel knew his stuff, and she was proud to be working with him. He was working hard at getting her things back to her that Phil had stolen, and some extras. While he'd not been left anything in the will, he had accumulated some really nice things by stealing from Grandda while he'd been alive. Things that she was going to get because of the stress that he had put her under.

She was getting better every day. Stronger too. She'd been using the treadmill at the condo at Kahana's home, and it had been working out well for her. Her once-a-week appointments with the heart specialist were down to once every other week, and that made her feel good, too. It had been a long road to recovery, but she was getting there step by step.

"I'm going to be picking up some medical

records to take with me. Mostly, the emergency room visit on that first day you were brought in. That's going to show the duress that he put you under, as well as the hospital. Not that I'm putting them all together, but they will be brought up when we talk about your having a heart attack at such a young age." She said that she would sign off on anything that he needed, so long as she could keep getting what was left to her. "Good. The other attorneys are signing off on the will today, and that will give you access to everything that came to you through the right will. That means you'll have to meet up with them in order to sign the deeds as well. I hope you don't mind, but I told them that Kahana was to be put on the deeds as well. Did you still want that to happen?"

"I did, and thank you for remembering. I'm supposed to go to the bank tomorrow and sign off on all the properties and accounts that he has, too. It seems to me like we both own places all over the world. I wonder what we'll do with them." Axel told her that most of them were rentals for both of them. "He said that he has extra income coming in, enough so that neither of us has to work. I don't know that I could become a lady of leisure. I'm more of a get-it-done kind of girl."

"So is my brother. Our grandmother, who is still in jail by the way, never could understand why we all wanted an education when we had enough money to buy ourselves into anything that we wanted. As you can imagine, we don't get along with her all that well. She's my dad's mother and hates our mom." She said that she'd heard about her through the others. "Yeah, she's not making things any better at the jail for the officers there either. I guess she expects them to go to Columbus and get her a fine meal with a bottle of wine. Of course, you can guess how that's going over."

"I can guess, yes." They worked for another two hours, and she was just about ready to go back home to take her nap when he told her about some money that was coming her way soon. "Is it part of the estate?"

"Yes and no. It's an insurance policy that your grandda took out on himself when he was in his twenties. It's worth quite a bit of money. Your grandmother had been the beneficiary up until about ten years ago, and now it's you. That's another thing that Phil tried to take from you when he was stealing your funds." She asked him how much it was worth. "Four million dollars. He would have paid on it for nearly sixty years when he took it out. The policy is coming to you today, along with some other insurance that he had. You'll be able to deposit whatever you need into an account that only you and Kahana can get to. I set it up that way so that Phil, if he gets out, won't be able to touch any of it."

"I like that idea. Keeping him away from my money is going to be a full-time job, I think." He agreed with her. "I'm headed home. My naps aren't as important as they were at the start, but I still go home and lie down for about half an hour. I feel better when I get up."

"Then by all means do what you need to do." He had her sign off on one more deed, and then she left. On her way to the new house, all she could do was marvel at how lovely it was.

They had moved into it last night after getting all her grandda's things moved out. He had quite a few suits that she donated to the shelter, so they could give them to people looking for a job. There were other things that she was going to donate when she got to them, but today she was going home to rest.

Yesterday she'd met with the other attorneys who were taking care of the will and the estate of her granddas. They were a nice group of people, if not a little overwhelmed about how much there was to go over. While they were taking care that everything that was to come to her didn't have any leans on it from Phil, they were also making sure to give her any information about the item or property, like pictures and such, so that she had a better idea what she was getting. She had files on everything, and it was nice to be able to put a picture with the item that they were talking about when they gave it to her.

"I was just thinking about you." She kissed Kahana, and he pulled her in for a nice hug. "I have to go back to work in a little bit. I have a woman in the beginning stages of labor, and I want to be there for her. Have you given any more thought as to which bedroom you want to share with me? No worries if you haven't. Axel told me that the two of you got a lot done today. That's fantastic."

"We did get a lot done. I've been putting your name on the deeds as well. Tomorrow I have an appointment with the banker, Mr. Bean, at eleven thirty. He said it should only take about an hour to get things signed. Are you sure you want to do that?" Kahana said that he loved her and wanted her to have everything that he did. "Same with me, but I never knew that my grandda was so diverse in things. He had his hand in just about everything, I believe."

"He does have a vast portfolio. Axel said that he took good notes on things that he had invested in as well. He said that he's learning things from this estate that he never would have thought of before." She told him about the pictures she was getting with each file. "That's a wonderful idea, too. This firm is living up to its reputation very well. That's probably why the state chose them to go over the accounts when Phil got into them. Have they found anything that he messed with that is going to cost a great deal of money to fix?"

"Not so far, they haven't. But I think they're about finished with it. They had thirty days to get it straightened out, and they're about there now. I was just telling Axel I'm sure that they're overwhelmed as much as I am about all the things that came to me." He kissed her again. "I've been thinking about some of the things that we talked about, and I want to have my grandda's room cleaned out, and we can share that room. It's big enough for the two of us to share. And there is plenty of closet space for whatever we need in there as well. I'm not up for the task, so if you know anyone who can do it, please let me know, and I'll get them started on it right away."

There were more questions that she had for Kahana, one of them being about sex. If she was honest about it, she was terrified to have sex with her heart still on the mend. She still remembered that pain like it was yesterday and didn't want to go through that again. But she didn't know how to bring it up without sounding whiny. She wanted to sleep with him and to make love to him, but she didn't want to die in the process. There had to be some way to talk to someone about it. She figured that today might be the day before they got too much more into getting things settled between them.

"Kahana, we never talked about sex." He smiled

at her, and she had to turn away. "I mean, I want to make love with you, but I'm…is there anything that I should do differently during sex?"

"What do you mean?" She knew that he would need more details and was frustrated when she couldn't put her finger on just how to ask him. "Are you asking me if you can have sex now that you've had a heart attack?"

"Yes." She was so relieved that she nearly passed out. As it was, she had to sit down with her head between her knees before she did. "I've been trying to ask you about it for days now, but didn't know how. Then I was going to ask my heart doctor, but he always seems so rushed when he's talking to me. I usually take notes with me, and I can barely get through them before he's off and running again. I like him, I do, but he's not much help when I have lots of questions. I usually want to scream at him to slow down before he has a heart attack of his own."

She saw his feet when she lifted her head a little, but didn't rise up. Being embarrassed made her do silly things, and hiding herself away like she was usually made her uncomfortable, too. Debra sat up when he asked her to.

"First of all, that's a good question, and shame on your doctor for not taking the time to talk to you. That should be his number one priority to talk to you about your questions and concerns." She said she wasn't really complaining about him. "You should. And while I won't have a talk with him, I'm going to see if that's the norm for his office. I should hope not."

"His nurses usually answer all my questions when I think about them. I do take notes with things on them, but I get so flustered when I have to chase down my answers. I guess I am complaining about him. I didn't mean to." Kahana said it was all right that she should complain about someone who wasn't helping her. "Thanks. I thought it was all about me. And perhaps he didn't think that I'm important enough to sit and talk to. Do you suppose he'd talk to me if I demanded him to sit down?"

"I don't know him all that well. I just know that he's one of the leading heart specialists in the country. That doesn't mean he has a good bedside manner, but he is good at what he does." She asked him about his manner around patients. "I do find myself rushing through talking to them at times, but when I do, I usually go back and talk to them more. It's a habit that I'm trying to break, seeing patients in a rush."

"So what about sex?" He told her that, sadly, she'd have to talk to her heart doctor. "I thought you'd say that. I made myself an appointment for tomorrow morning. I asked for two slots so that I could get some of the other questions that I have answered. Like, sometimes I'm dizzy when I wake up. That could be normal, but I don't know."

"Take your list and tell him when he comes into the room that you have a list of questions you need answers to. Also, tell his nurse so that she can give him a heads up when he comes to see you. Don't skip around on your questions. Ask him all of them and get answers until you're clear about them. Don't just think you understand. You need to understand and make it clear to him. If he still wants to fob you off, then we'll find another doctor who will answer everything for you." She asked what happens if he doesn't want to be her doctor anymore. "Then he won't be. There are other specialists around that can help you and some that would be willing to answer your questions so that you don't feel rushed or put off."

They talked about her list, and she realized that she was asking the same question over again in some of them. Kahana helped her sort through them and was even able to answer a couple of her concerns himself. He said that while he wasn't a heart doctor, he did know symptoms about the heart that she could use. In the end, she told him how much better she felt just knowing that it wasn't her who needed answers, but that most people did when they suffered a heart attack like she had.

When he left her to deliver a baby, she could

almost feel jealous of him bringing a new life into the world. She laid down on her bed and thought about her morning tomorrow and wondered if she should have just made one appointment a day. She didn't want to get stressed out again and was working very hard on not being that way, but there were times when she just wanted to say fuck it and do what needed to be done to get it finished. Then she'd remember the pain, and that would have her pacing herself again. When people said that stress was a killer, they really had no idea how true that was. She didn't want to die and didn't want to suffer another attack either. And it was going to be up to her that it didn't happen.

Chapter 4

Hanna didn't like all this going on around her. She should have been put on the bus by herself and not had to go to the courthouse with all these people. They were criminals, the lot of them, and she didn't feel the need to be around them. Charles, her son, was going to pay for this, and she was going to get to that wife of his, too.

"Damned people." All she had wanted was more money in order to live the life that she deserved. Her damned husband had left everything to their son so that nothing came to her but an allowance. Like she was five years old or something. Well, she was going to get as much as she wanted if she had to knock a few heads together to get it. "They took my damned guns, and I want them back."

She'd meant to kill Dani off, Charles' wife, and that damned kid of theirs, Mackenzie. They actually tossed her out of the house as if she wasn't there to set the record straight. Then they told her that the retirement place she'd been staying had kicked her to the curb, and they'd moved all her things into storage of all things.

"Like they could run that place without me there to set the record straight. Damned people." One of the inmates on the bus with her tried to have a conversation with her. She ignored him. She wasn't a criminal, and that sort of person was beneath her. But he wouldn't leave her alone.

"You're the woman who wants fine dining while in a jail cell. I hear you bitching all the time." She told him she wasn't bitching at all but trying to get them to treat her with the respect that she deserves. "You're in jail. You'll have to give up on respect. People no longer will treat you like a person now that you've been behind bars."

"What do you know? I'm a well-respected person of wealth, and I get things done." He told her that she was still eating the food that he did. "As soon as my son gets his head out of his ass, then I'll have that and more. What do you care anyway? You've probably never done a day's work in your life."

"Oh, I work hard at being what I am. It took me a long time to forge the will for my grandda. Fat lot of good it did me. Debra still won anyway, but I'm going to get back at her today. See that I don't." He laughed. "She tried to pay me off with a measly million dollars when I know that she has billions. My grandda left it all to her. A woman to have fun with. And then she tells me that I have to get away from her from now on, like I'm not her only living relative. What the fuck is up with that?"

"If I had my cane, I'd hit you with it. Didn't your grandda teach you any manners and not speak like that in front of your elders? You should be ashamed of yourself." He said that the only thing he was ashamed of was getting caught. "Yes, well, my only regret is that I didn't go into the house with both guns blazing and kill the lot of them. Don't think I will make that mistake again. Even that granddaughter of mine. She should have been killed when they first created her. Damned upstart. I'll show her too when I get out of here. And they'd better have my stuff back where it was. Can you imagine them going into my home and touching my things? Then they used my money to pay the bills that I purposely didn't pay because I am above such things. Damned people."

They were at the courthouse in no time at all. They could have taken them over in one of the police cars, and it would have been nicer. Cooler for sure. These people were starting to get on her last nerve, and when she was backed into a corner like she was, she came out with her guns. People underestimated her one time, then never again.

Chained up like a dog, she was seated next to the man who had been chatty with her. Not that she liked talking to his sort, but he did while away the time so that she wasn't as pissed off when she arrived. It was important to her to show her best side, and she'd been reminded before that being pissed off at the judge wasn't a smart way to go. She didn't want to be fined right out of the start when she needed her son there to see that she wasn't going to be taking his shit either.

The odor around the convicts was strong, and she was going to need her smelling salts before too much longer. Telling the others to back away from her did very little good as they were chained together like a string of lights on a Christmas tree. And she was the only bright bulb in the group.

Hanna wondered how it had come to her being in jail when she was the rock of so many things. Ten minutes with her around and things would not only run better, but they'd be making more money too. And all she wanted out of it was their devotion to her in the form of money. No one knew the things that she had to go through just to have a few bucks stashed away for a rainy day. By her estimations, she should have had about four hundred thousand dollars stashed away in her place, and it had better be just where she left it, too, or someone was going to pay. That damned granddaughter of hers was on her list, and no one wanted to be on her list for very long. Mackenzie had been on her list since she first saw the mongrel. She would have been better served being a stain on the sheets than a granddaughter of hers.

They were taking people off the string of them into the courtroom one at a time. She wasn't supposed to go first because of something about her being second to last in being arrested. If they didn't have time to listen to her today, she'd have to be the first one next time the judge came through, and that just wasn't going to happen. It was going to be today, by god, or heads were going to be rolling.

"Excuse me, I have important matters that need to be attended to." The chatty man snorted, and she tried her best to ignore him. "I want to go in there now and have my turn. I've been locked up long enough, and I want my son to come bail me out."

"It's not your turn. You'll be gotten to soon, but not next." The officer said she was fifth in line, and that was the way it went. "When it's your turn, you'll have your say. Not that I think anyone cares. You've been spouting off your complaints for the last two weeks, and we're all frankly sick of hearing them. If I had my way, I would have put you first so that you'd be out of my hair, but I don't make the rules."

"I make the rules around here, and you're going to be doing what I said. Put me in line next, or so help me I'll snatch you bald. Do you understand me?" He said that he did, but just didn't care what she said. "What a thing to say to me. I demand to be put in front of these others, or so help me, I'll have your job."

"Take it. See how much fun it is wrangling inmates like you all day." He unhooked the person next to her and told them they were next. "You keep bitching like you are, and you'll be last, not fourth like you are now."

She wanted her gun. At the very least, she wanted her cane so that she could knock some sense into the man. There was no way that her taxes — if she ever paid them, were paying this man a wage to treat her like this. If she'd had her way, she would have fired him on the spot and done what she wanted. But without her weapons of choice, she was left to the treatment of those around her. Damned people. She hated them all.

When it was her turn to go into the courtroom, the first thing she did was look for her son and his ungrateful family. If they only knew what she did on a daily basis, they'd have a great deal more respect for her. Just as she was going to ask the judge where they were, they lot of them came into the room from the back. She was disappointed to see that milksop of a wife next to her grandson, Charles. Then she saw Mackenzie.

"I don't want her in here. She's mouthy and will cause a disruption by pissing me off more than I already am." The judge told her to watch her language.

"I will not. I know my rights."

"Oh, I've heard about you. You're the woman who keeps calling my office demanding things that are well above the norm for an inmate." She said that she should have what she wanted, as people knew better than to say no to her. "Well, aren't you just a bucket of sunshine. The word no is going to be said a lot, I'm afraid to warn you. Now, let's get down to business."

"I refuse to listen to you with that thing in here." He told her that she only had to nod once in a while that she was getting it, and that was his rules. "I don't care for your rules. I have my own set that are far above anything that you might say to me."

"This will go a good deal faster if you can keep your mouth shut." He started reading off all the things that she'd been brought before the court for. Some of them were petty things like not paying her bills on time or at all, but the one about back taxes got her standing up again. "You have something to say about owning the government some money?"

"I don't have a job, so how do I have to pay taxes to a government that has done nothing for me?" He explained that she had income from her son's estate. "It's not his anything. That should have been mine if my stupid husband had done right by me. He left it all to that cur of a son there and only gives me a small stipend each month that I'm supposed to be happy with."

"You had more than six hundred thousand dollars stashed around your home. And from what I understand, you never paid anything for where you were living, nor anything else that I can find. Did you really tell the paperboy that you were to get the newspaper for free because you paid your taxes? You do know that the government doesn't have anything to do with the newspaper that you were getting for free, don't you?"

"I know the laws better than you do." She saw the shocked look on his face and was happy that she'd been able to put it there. "I want you to demand that my son and so-called wife pay me more money. And while we're on the subject of money, I want all the money back that I had saved in my condo. They had no right to touch that, as it was mine."

"You have a lot of demands for someone who is chained to the floor like a convict. Which, by the way, you are." He laughed at her, and she saw red. Her head was hurting her so bad right now that she couldn't see straight. Everything was in a haze for her, and she was going to be sick. It would serve them right if she were to just lean over and puke up that sham of a breakfast that she'd had this morning. "I'm taking a twenty-minute break so that you can compose yourself in a better manner. After that, I'm going to figure out the best time to have a court hearing against you. For what I've seen of your actions today, it's left no doubt in my mind that everything that has been said about you is true."

He was gone before she could form her next demand. The bastard just walked away from her like she was nothing. Well, by god, she'd show him. When he came back, she was going to demand that he do right by her and let her go. She had people to knock around, and they might even end up dead. She'd had enough of being the nice person in all this.

Hanna was told to sit down, and she had to. Not that their ordering her to do so had anything to do with it. She was sick with a headache, and she wanted something for it. She knew what would cure it. A nice fat payday from her son, as well as her guns back. She'd had to work hard at getting them, and she wasn't happy that someone had taken them from her when she had plans. She was going to make her son do what she wanted, or she was going to simply kill him. Something that she should have done when he was just a baby. Damn it, she just wanted things to go her way for a change.

By the time the judge came back, she was sick. Her chest was crushing her, and she had a feeling that she wasn't going to be better until she saw a doctor. Damned people would rob her blind, too; she knew how they were. When told to stand up, she couldn't do it. There was just too much pain in her body for her to do much of anything but be in pain.

"I think I need a doctor." She slumped forward in her chair, and if not for the chains on her, she would have fallen on her face. As it was, she was having a hard time thinking, too. Just as she was beginning to think that all was lost, she felt herself being laid on the floor. "You're going to get me dirty, damn it."

In her mind, that's what she said, but it sounded gibberish to her. Someone was asking her questions about medications, and all she could think about was that they cost money that she didn't want to spend. The pain was getting worse, and it was all she could do not to cry. But that would be undignified, so she didn't let herself do that. But she could feel the tears rolling down her face as someone spoke above her. She didn't know what they were saying, but for whatever reason, she thought it was important. Closing her eyes against the pain, she felt her heart break.

~*~

"I'm so sorry for your loss, Charles. I want you to know that I did everything that I could to save her." Charles said that he knew that, too. "I've spoken to her doctor, and he said that she was a time bomb just waiting to go off. She should have been taking better care of herself, he told me."

"She more than likely thought that she'd live forever, knowing her the way that I do." Charles sat down, then stood up again. "I should do something, but for the life of me, I can't think of a single thing that needs my attention. It's like I expect her to come through that door and tell me what an ungrateful cur I am. That was her favorite thing to call me was a cur. I wonder what she was thinking when she didn't take her meds like she should have been."

"Like you said, she more than likely thought that she was going to live forever. At least outlive you." He didn't know what to say to the older man but how sorry he was. "Had she been in a hospital setting, I might have had the equipment to bring her back. But I fear her quality of life wouldn't have been all that good."

"I have to admit that I'm sort of relieved that she's gone. I know that's a horrible thing for someone to think about their own mother, but the thought of her not being around bothering me anymore is a blessing." He said that he understood. "Yes, I suppose you would. You're a good man, Kahana, and I'm glad that you were there for her when she died. She's really gone, isn't she?"

"Yes, she's gone." They talked about the arrangements that needed to be made, and then he asked him if he'd thought about what he was going to do now. "I mean, the trial will still go as planned so that a lot of people can get their closure. Her money will go to compensating those people that she wronged as well."

"I cut ties with her years ago. I made it legally binding that her debts were her own and had nothing to do with me. I think that made her angriest of all, me telling her that I wanted nothing to do with the debt that she incurred. She believed that she should have been able to charge anything she wanted or deserved back to me, and I wasn't having it."

"Smart man. I'm betting that Axel would tell you the same thing." He said he'd told him about it when they'd been gathering evidence about her activities. "I'm betting that he tells more people about that when he has a chance as well. I know that I would be."

"Is she really gone, Kahana? I know that I keep asking you that, but I just can't wrap my mind around her being dead. She's been a terrible part of my life for so long that I find that I can't think beyond her being around to upset me again." He told him that she was well and truly gone. "Good. I'm beginning to feel better about that, too. She didn't die of a heart attack, but plain and pure meanness. It's small wonder that she lived as long as she did with as mean as she was. I swear there isn't a person around that will mourn her passing." He looked at him. "I'm sorry. I can't believe

I said that to you."

"That's all right. I understand. You do realize, for as much as I disliked her, I tried my best to save her the other day." He said that he did understand that, yes. "Good. I don't want there to be any question later about how I didn't try my best. I treated her like every other patient that I see."

"I know that. You're a good man and a better doctor." They shook hands, and then Charles hugged him. "My life will be better from now on. I didn't realize how tense she made me feel all the time. And while she was in jail, I felt a little more at ease because I knew that she couldn't get to me. Isn't that terrible to think of your own mother that way?"

"No. She brought it all on herself." Charles agreed. He didn't mind him repeating himself all the time. He'd been given a great blow, and he wanted to be there for him. If it took him repeating his questions to him for him to help, then that's what he'd do. He'd answer them like he'd never heard them before, each and every time. "Have you decided what you're going to do about a funeral? I'm to understand that she didn't have a will made out either."

"There was a will, but it was made when I was just a little boy. It has who was to care for me in the event that she died before I turned into an adult. But the rest is the same. She didn't have anything unless my dad provided it to her, so she had nothing to leave. There isn't even an insurance policy. I don't think she planned on ever dying. Or at least she planned to outlive me." Kahana said he was sorry about that. "Don't be. I was lucky in that I had a wonderful wife as well as two of the best children. Charlie and Milly have made me a grandda, and Mac is married now, so there might be children from her union. I couldn't be more proud of the people they married either. Axel and Milly are just like my own children when it comes to them being part of my family. Yes, I'm a very lucky man."

"Yes, you are. We had the best parents growing up. We've always had money, but it was never anything that we tried to shove in anyone's face. They taught us to be appreciative of the things that we had so that if anything happened, we wouldn't be relying on family money to make our daily bread. I think that they're the reason that we've all worked so hard to become more than just a bunch of rich bastards that didn't give a shit about their fellow man." Charles said that he did notice that they all worked hard at something they were fond of. "Yes. I love being a doctor. I know that Axel loves being an attorney now that he's out on his own. Same with the rest of my brothers."

"I know that your brother Penrod is a homicide detective and that Gilman is an electrical engineer.

Also, Stamos is a journalist. I don't think I ever knew what Audon does for a living. I see him around, but I don't know that I've actually seen or heard what he does." He told him. "An artist? You don't say. Have I seen some of his work?"

"I'm sure you have if you've been in the bank. That's his mural on the walls as you get inside. Also, the mayor's offices. He has showings all over the world that bring in people from everywhere. He's really good and loves it." He said he was going to have to pay more attention when he went to those places. "He's done some of the paintings at my parents' home, too. Those are just for them, and they hang them with pride. When I get my house finished, I'm going to have him give me a few of his pieces that I can display around for when people come over. I'm very proud of him."

"It sounds like it." The two of them talked about Audon while they stood in line to get a cup of tea from the vendor right outside the courthouse. Kahana had been there filing the death certificate for Hanna after her autopsy was finished. "I didn't drink tea all that much until recently. I guess Mac drinks it with Axel, and I've gotten in the habit from her. I never realized how good it can be with a muffin in the morning."

"I don't drink too much of the caffeinated tea. It keeps me up. And as a doctor, I need to be able to sleep when I can get it in the event that I'm called out. I get those on occasion." He told him about the baby that he'd delivered just the other day. "Beautiful little boy, and both mom and son are going home today. That's the best part of my job, delivering babies."

"It would be mine as well, I think." The two of them talked about their jobs. Charles had recently retired, leaving all the business to Mac. He could still be found on job sites on occasion, but mostly he worked from home when Mac needed him. Charlie, his older boy, had his own job and didn't want anything to do with the construction end of the business. He had a baby girl due any day now, with a son at home already. "I'm looking forward to the holidays this year. No more mom coming in at the last moment and spoiling things for us all. She would say she wasn't coming and get our hopes all up, then she'd just show up the morning of Christmas and demand that we all cater to her. She was a nightmare."

It didn't take long for the two of them to talk about his own wife-to-be and the holidays. Kahana was looking forward to this year because it would be the first in his forever home. They were already looking at decorations, and it was still July. His parents always hosted Thanksgiving, and he knew that this year was going to be the biggest it's ever been with the two new wives and their families. But Axel wanted to host Christmas, and it was all being planned. He couldn't wait until they came around so that they could all celebrate the holidays with style.

On his rounds this morning, he was a little preoccupied with some of the questions he was being asked. Nothing really serious, but something he was going to have to give some thought to. One of the professors at the university asked if he would mind if the upcoming doctors followed him around in the mornings to get practice. He usually had them done by nine in the morning, but today, with the students, it was taking him much longer. They were asking him questions that he didn't think or even know what he should be doing. Like, did he have a routine.

Did he? He had no idea. He just picked up the first file that the nurses laid out for him and went from there. If he had a routine, he would say that his was to depend on the staff because they were the closest to the patients all the time and knew them much better than he did. He relied on them a great deal.

After finishing up with the students, he made his way to the office. He usually had patients to deal with there, as he was more of a general practitioner. They would come to see him there rather than go to the hospital for things. He could stitch a person up and handle the flu. Also, he was a good OBGYN, or baby doctor.

After work, he walked home. He was glad for

the time between work and home. It let him unwind a good bit before tackling whatever had to be done at home. He'd forgotten that Debra wasn't going to be at home as she was going to the jail to see her cousin about the offer she'd made him a week ago. Also, he was being remanded over to the bigger prison to await his trial date, and he wasn't happy about that. Kahana couldn't care less what he liked and disliked. He'd been a pain in the ass since he'd met Debra.

He was forever having someone call the house to talk to Debra. He noticed that it was stressing her out again and suggested that she have the jail stop calling her at home. It worked out for a while, then the police started calling home for her to come in and talk to him. He was getting out of hand, and he was glad that he wasn't going to be around for much longer were they had to put up with him anymore. He slowed his steps when he noticed a car in the driveway that he didn't know. Knowing that Debra wasn't home made him feel better, but he still didn't know who was at their home.

Going into the house, he was surprised to find Charlie there. He usually came over in a minivan with his family, so he didn't know it was him until he was inside. After greeting the man with a hug and handshake, he asked him what he could do for him. The man was great to be around; he never seemed to be upset about anything.

"I told Milly that I'd come by and see you on the way home today. She and I can't travel back home yet as she's having contractions. She wanted to know if you would deliver our little girl for us when the time came. She doesn't know any of the doctors around here and would feel better to have someone she knows there when it's time." He said he'd be honored to. "She usually has quick labors, at least she did with our son. I'm looking forward to having our daughter born so that we can be a family of four. What do you need from us so that you can do it? I have her doctor's name and phone number. That should get you her files."

"That's about all I need for now. After I look over the files, I'll be better prepared to ask questions. Did she know what sort of epidural she wants?" After getting a few questions unanswered, Charlie called his wife. Kahana was prepared as he'd ever been on a delivery after getting off the phone with the wife. "I'll call your doctor right now and have the file faxed over to me. It's no problem at all for me to do this for you two."

"We were kind of nervous about this happening. I'm glad we can depend on you." Kahana said he was happy to be able to do it. "Good. I'll tell her it's all going to be all right, so she doesn't stress anymore. There is nothing wrong with Milly, but she has been nervous about this since we got here."

After assuring him that things would be fine, the younger man went home. He was really happy to be able to do this for them and thought it was nice that they'd asked. He'd never delivered a relative's child before and was looking forward to it. He did a little dance around the office before calling the doctor. He had nothing but good things to say about Milly and her upcoming delivery.

Chapter 5

"I told you that the money was only good for twenty-four hours, then the deal is off. I don't care that you think you're going to have to grease paws while in prison. I don't even know what that means, do you?" Phil told her what he meant. "Like you're going to be able to carry around cash all the time. And if you think that I'm going to visit you while you're there, you're nuttier than a fruit cake. I'm finished with you."

Debra thought that she was handling herself quite well today. She'd not had a nap or needed one for the last several days, and she knew that she was sleeping better at night. After talking with her doctor this morning, she was feeling a great deal better about a lot of things, not just getting her cousin out of her life. He spoke again, and she had to have him repeat himself.

"Pay attention to me. I said I want you to set it up so that I have funds when I need them. I don't want you to nickel and dime me either. You put some real money in my account so that I can get what I want when I want it. I'm not kidding you right now, Debra. I want you to take care of me." She didn't say anything to him but let him go on and on. "And I want that million dollars you promised me. It looks like I might be in here for a while, and I want things that I need. I'm going to have to pay someone so that I can have a cell phone to remind you daily of what you need to do for me."

"I'm not doing anything for you. I told you three times now that the million dollars is no longer on the table. I really dodged the bullet with that one. I don't have to pay you, and you're still going away for a long time." She smiled at him when he called her a cunt. "Be nice to me, or I'll leave. Not that I plan on doing anything for you, but you will be nice to me."

"I wish every day that I'd never had a cousin like you." She told him that she wished the same thing about him daily. "So we're even on that score. But that doesn't mean that you're going to—"

"How do you know all this about prison? I mean, as far as I know, you've never been behind bars, much less in prison, where you belong. How do you know that you're going to need to grease palms or whatever you called it? Or, for that matter, having a cell phone? Maybe they have one there for you that you can use? Are you watching those prison shows that show people who are there for life? That sounds like something that you'd rely on for your information." She snorted at him. "Next thing you'll tell me is that you know who you're going to be inmates with. Do they really put all of you in one bedroom so that you have no privacy? That alone would keep me from doing anything that might cause me to have to go away. I couldn't stand not having my own things around me."

"What are you talking about?" She shrugged at him and told him she was thinking about prison life. "Why? Are you planning on joining me? That would be a hoot. Little Miss Debra Author behind bars. You're never one to have a little bit of fun."

"And look where that's gotten you, having your little bit of fun. No thanks. I'll be a good citizen and watch myself. You go on being the jailbird." That pissed him off, and she found his anger funny. She thought that she was dealing with him much better than she had been about a month ago. Now she knew to not let him get to her. She also knew what she had to do when he was getting to her, and even that was coming to her more easily.

While he was still going on about the money offer, she thought about the conversation she'd had with her doctor just this morning. He had actually stopped to talk to her this morning, and she was glad. She didn't know what she would have done if he had rushed her through like he had been. He even apologized to her that he'd not been taking his time like he should have. She wondered if Kahana had said something to him or one of his nurses. She had complained a little to them about not getting her questions answered when in the office with him.

They could have sex so long as they didn't swing from the lights. She'd been embarrassed a little when he said that, and that made him laugh. He told her that he should have made it clear to her that she could do whatever she had done before, so long as it was in moderation. And that she watched her diet.

"Eating right will be the best thing for you. I know you told me that you're walking every day, and that's the best way to go. You can lift a little bit of weights, but don't strain yourself." She said that she'd been doing chair yoga. "Whatever you do to strengthen your muscles is great." She also asked him about her medications and how they were making her have a little bit of an upset stomach. "We can try something else if you want. I'd tell you to give it a bit more time, as your body is making all kinds of adjustments as it's getting used to this new you. But you let me know when you've had enough of it, and we'll switch it out for something else. I'm willing to do anything to keep you healthy."

"Are you even listening to me?" she told Phil that she'd had enough listening to him and wondered when he was going to be finished. "I'm not going to be finished until you help me with this list they gave me.

Then I might allow you to leave."

"You do understand that I'm not the one who is chained up, don't you? I can leave you at any time." She looked at the list that he'd been going over. "There is nothing on here that says anything about greasing palms. I think you made that part up."

"If I were free right now, I'd slap the shit out of you. Of course, they're not going to tell you that part. And I did watch it on television. There is all kinds of information you can get out there when you have the time." She told him he'd not be in this situation if he'd used his time more productively. "Had you just stayed out of my business, none of this would have happened in the first place. I should have had the estate, and you should be living on the streets someplace. What about the firm? Have you sold it yet?"

"As a matter of fact, I did." He said that he wanted half of the money since it had been his idea. "Yours? I don't think so. You were going to run it in the ground. I sold it to the partners so that they could call it whatever they wanted. As of right now, I don't have to worry about it anymore, and I'm going to be my own attorney."

"That sounds boring. Why would you want to work for yourself when there are so many people out there willing to hire you?" He snorted at her. "You're just a girl and a stupid one at that. Debra, I demand that you give me my part in the estate so that I can have an easier life in prison. It's the least you can do for me since you took everything from me. In fact, I blame you for even being sent to prison in the first place."

"Good. I feel like I did one good deed by getting you off the streets." She stood up to leave, and he bitched at her. "I'm going home. I've had enough of you yelling at me for no reason. If you were nicer, I might have set you up an account, but I'm not going to do that. I have better things to do with my money than to help you enjoy your prison life. I want you to suffer every day like you made me."

"So help me, I'm going to make you suffer worse than you are now." She said that was funny since she wasn't suffering at all anymore. "I'm not finished with you yet. You sit down until we get this resolved. I want the money that you promised me."

"You turned it down, remember?" He told her that he wasn't going to prison back then. "I told you that you were going. You should have listened to me. You never were very bright, were you?"

As she made her way down the hallway out of the room they'd been given for talking, she thought about how she was going to spend the rest of her life. She was going to be happy with Kahana and his family if it was the last thing that she did. And she was going to start out her life of having fun by jumping the bones of the good doctor as soon as she could.

While she was still nervous about sex with him, she had it in her head that he'd be as gentle as he could be with her. Knowing her fears, he'd make love to her slowly and without swinging from the light poles either.

She was excited that he was home when she got there. While he was on the phone, she figured out dinner tonight. They were having pork chops on the grill with potatoes. She couldn't have a large potato, but she was looking forward to the chops. Their new cook was helping with her diet well, and she loved her for it. Kahana found her in the kitchen, where she was having a snack of fresh veggies before dinner. He took two of her carrots and ate them while he told her about Millie's baby.

"I've spoken to her doctor already, and he's fine with me delivering her. I have an appointment tomorrow with Millie and Charlie in the morning to make sure that things are progressing as well as they could be." She told him about her visit with Phil and how she had not been the least bit upset by his demands. "That's wonderful news. I knew you could do it."

She told him about everything that he'd said, especially about him wanting to grease palms and how she'd made fun of him. The cell phone wasn't going to happen unless he could get someone to sneak it in for him, and she didn't think he had any friends who were willing to risk jail time over a cell phone.

"Not to mention me setting him up a fund so that he can grease palms. I'm not even sure how that would work. Do you just tell the person in charge of your funds that you want to bribe someone with money from your account? I don't know where his mind is most of the time. He admitted to watching shows about prison life and that some of the things he was thinking were true. I don't know. I suppose he could be right, but I'm not going to help him." She looked at Kahana when he stole another carrot. "Do you suppose someone will make him their bitch, and all the money in the world wouldn't help him. I kind of hope that's what happens. That he learns the hard way what it's like to bully people around like he's done his entire life."

Kahana laughed and laughed. She didn't know what was so funny, but smiled at his getting such a kick out of whatever she said. As she finished up the last of her treat, she put the plate in the sink and took his hand into hers. It was time that they had a conversation about the doctor, and she didn't want to do it in front of the cook.

Taking him to his office, she sat across from him in one of the big chairs and told him everything that had happened at the office. Her blood pressure was at an all-time low, and her blood work had come back all normal. Then she told him what he'd said about them having sex.

"He said that he knew you well enough that you'd be gentle with me. I wasn't sure how to take that, but I agreed. And he told me that at any time I was overwhelmed, all I had to say was to stop, and you would. Why does he know this?" He said they'd been friends for a very long time. "Good. I thought that might be the case, but I didn't know. Do you want to have sex later? I'm still kind of nervous about it, but I know you'd never hurt me."

"Not for anything in the world." She nodded at him and felt her eyes fill with tears. "I love you, Debra. With all my heart. I'd never do anything with you or to you without you being willing."

"I know that too." He stood up and came around the side of the desk she was at. Getting down on his knees, he walked to her that way until he was in front of her. When he laid his head on her lap, she curled her fingers into his hair and marveled at how soft it was. "I love you, Kahana. So very much."

"Will you marry me? As soon as it can be arranged?" She told him she'd marry him today if it were possible. "Good. I have a ring for you. I was going to take you with me when I went to pick it out, but I saw this one and knew it was perfect for you."

He sat up and slipped the ring on her finger. She couldn't believe how beautiful it was and how it shone with small diamond patterns around the room as she admired it. Pulling her down to his mouth, he kissed her thoroughly and with passion. She could taste it when he tangled his tongue around hers when she gave him access. Spreading her legs open, he pulled her flush with his body, and she wrapped her legs around his waist. Every part of her body seemed to tense up until he spoke to her.

"I have you. I'm not going to hurt you." She nodded. "I want to make love to you right here on the floor, but I'm going to take you up to bed and take you there. It will be the best night of our long life together."

The knock at the door had him cursing. When they were called to dinner, she giggled. He put his forehead onto hers and sighed heavily. She thought it was the funniest thing in the world and told him so. When he rocked into her, letting her feel his cock, she moaned.

"It's going to be difficult to walk around as hard as I am. You're going to pay for this." She asked him what she'd done. "You said yes."

They made their way into the kitchen to have dinner. They'd been eating in this room since they moved in. As soon as they were seated, he took her smaller hand into his and kissed the back of it. She'd never felt anything sexier in her life.

~*~

He knew she was nervous after dinner, and they went to the living room. It was their favorite part of the house and a room they spent a great deal of time in. Giving her room on the couch, they talked about their day again, and he told her how excited he was to be delivering Millie's baby. Almost as soon as he finished telling her for the second time tonight how happy he was, she laid her head on his shoulder. She was asleep in no time.

Kahana didn't dare move because he didn't want to disturb her. While she slept, he dozed off and on, thinking about how much he loved her. When she shivered a little, he pulled the blanket off the back of the couch and covered them both up. He was falling asleep even as he realized how exhausted he was and happy to have her beside him.

When he woke up to his cell phone going off, he answered it with his name. As soon as he heard Millie talking to someone else, he knew what had happened. There would be no doctor's appointment in the morning; she was going to have her baby tonight.

"My water broke. I'm not in hard labor yet, but I can feel the contractions are getting harder." He told her to go to the hospital and that he'd meet them there.

"Is everything going to be all right? I didn't have my water break the first time."

"Everything is going to be fine. I'll meet you there." He moved his legs and discovered that Debra had stretched out over him with her head on the pillow and was awake. He told her what was going on. "Did you want to come with me? It won't be long, I've been told."

"Yes, of course." She hurriedly got up and pulled on her shoes. "I've never seen a newborn before. I'm excited that Millie's will be my first." The two of them talked as they got dressed to go. "Do we have to call anyone?"

"I have to call the hospital and have things ready for her. Other than that, I'm sure that Charlie has everything under control. He's very calming, isn't he?" Debra agreed and was dressed before he was. He would normally wear his street clothing into the hospital and change there, but today was different. He wanted to be ready to go when she was.

He made the calls while Debra drove them to the hospital. She'd go in through the emergency department, and they'd take her right up to Labor and Delivery. At least that was the plan when he called in to have her moved. As soon as they pulled up in front of the ER, he was out of the car and on his way to Millie and Charlie. It was nice that Debra said she'd park for them; it gave him extra time to get to where he was going.

Things were moving right along when he met them in the labor room. Millie would be in this room from now until she went home with her newborn. It was easier on the staff to know where she was going, and he liked the fact that it was all central to one room as well. He knew just where he was going when he got there.

"The contractions are moving right along, Millie. You'll have this baby by morning." She asked if he was sure everything was all right. "Why do you ask? Does this feel different than your other birth? It's all right if it does. All births are different."

"I feel bloated this time. Like I'm too big." He didn't know what that meant to her, so he had her clarify. "When Charles was born, I felt like I was just having a baby; the rest of me didn't get big. With this baby, I feel like I'm so swollen all the time. The doctor's been keeping an eye on me. He did tell me I was larger this time to expect a bigger baby than Charles was." She looked helpless. "I'm sorry. I'm not making any sense."

"You are. I understand. And I'll keep an eye on you as well. Had you waited like a good girl, I would have given you a thorough exam in the morning." He laughed with her. "We'll be just fine. I have a great staff here, and they're ready for most anything. How about I run an ultrasound for you and see if the baby is all right and get a guess on how big she is?"

"That would be great." She was starting labor now that she was in a good place to begin, and he carefully ran the scan over her swollen baby three times. "Is she all right?"

"She is. Her heart rate is a little fast, but I don't foresee a problem with that at the moment. Like I said, we'll keep an eye on the two of you. She's not large at all. She should be about six pounds. I think that's a good weight for you. She's head down and ready to come out and see you guys." Millie thanked him, and he had to smile. "You're acting like a good mom, and that's what we hope for on our end. You're going to be fine."

He told the staff what he wanted done, and they got on things immediately. The baby's bed was pulled out to get ready, as when examined, Millie was progressing faster than he'd expected. Things were going well, and he had things going in the event that things went south, as he always did. He didn't expect anything to go wrong, but he was never without that thought in his head.

At just after one in the morning, things were ready. Millie was ready to push, and Charlie was there to coach her through labor and delivery. Kahana was at his station, and he kept an eye on the monitors. The child's heart rate was still a little fast, but he was waiting for it to be born before he said anything. It was time to bring the little one into the world.

After the baby was born at one twenty, he could say that she was a healthy little thing, weighing six pounds and one ounce. Her Apgar was perfect at the onset, and he was thrilled with the way Millie was handling things. When she said that she had to push again, he didn't panic but watched as the head of a second child came into view.

"We're having twins." Millie said no, and Charlie looked like he might faint. "Did the doctor tell you that you were having twins? It wasn't mentioned in my paperwork."

"He said that there were two when I first got my first scan done, then he said it had been a mistake as he never saw her again." She pushed harder, and he delivered the baby. "Christ, I knew that I felt different."

Baby girl two was just as perfect as baby one. She weighed six pounds and three ounces, and her Apgar was perfect. They both had blonde hair and were the cutest little things he'd ever delivered. Of course, they were his first set of twins, too. Millie was stitched up and ready to hold her little ones when Charlie said he had a feeling that things weren't as set as he'd been told.

"I explained how twins had run in my family, and he said that Millie was too small to be carrying twins. I didn't know what that meant, and he didn't seem to be inclined to answer me." Kahana didn't say anything; he would never say anything against another doctor, but this could have been dangerous. Treating for twins might have saved Millie from feeling so bloated all the time. "I'm glad you were here to deliver them. There is no telling what he might have done had he been in the operating room with her. This is so much nicer. He would have had her delivering in an operating room rather than a cozy room like this one."

He didn't tell him that had he known there were twins, he might have done things differently. Millie was a small woman, and having twelve pounds of baby could have been hard on her. Not that things would have turned out perfect anyway, but with twins, you just never know what is going to happen when they're delivered.

Since he was acting as pediatrician for the babies, too, he ordered tests on them and was happy when some of the blood tests came back fine. Both girls were taken to the nursery, where they were cleaned up and examined, and he did the same for Millie. She was in great shape for a woman who had just delivered, and he was proud of how well she'd handled the second child coming along, in that she didn't seem the least bit surprised that she'd had twin girls.

"How could he miss an entire baby?" He said that sometimes one will hide behind the other, and that will cause him to miss one of them. "Is that the reason for the fast heartrate? You were listening to two of them? They told me when I went in for my last scan that the baby wasn't large and that there was a fast heartrate. I think I knew then and was going to tell you in the morning. Once I got here, I was too busy to think about anything but having a healthy little girl. Now I have twins." He told her that she was lucky in that. "I know that I am. We only wanted a boy and a girl. I'm so happy that I have the girls that I could bust. Charlie wanted a girl with Charles, but neither of us would trade him for the world."

"He's going to be happy about having two sisters." Millie said he was at the jealous age and might not care that there are two dividing his time with her and Dad. "He'll get over that soon enough. I'm sure that you've read how to combat those sorts of feelings. You're a smart mom."

"I have read all the books. I'm just happy that things are going to go well from now on. That other doctor was too old to be delivering babies in this time. His ideas were too old for what modern mothers want to have done. He told me to expect to stay five days in the hospital when I delivered so that the nurses could care for my little one. I want them right here with me all the time. I don't want to miss them." He just held her hand while she spoke, and when she kissed the back of it, he was a little startled until she explained. "You were wonderful. You never told me to be put under when I went into hard labor. That's the way that he does all his labor and delivery cases."

"I don't think you needed to be out. I like it when I can talk to my patients." She said that he'd done just what she'd wanted. "Good, then it was a success all the way around. Now you have to tell your parents that you have two little girls to spoil, and they'll be thrilled no matter how they came into the world."

"I can't wait. Charlie is going to talk to his dad first." She told him that things would go better that way than telling her parents. "They tend to go a little overboard. I'm so happy right now I could bust. Twin little girls. Can you believe it?"

He did and was happy that things were going so well for the young couple. He couldn't wait to have his own children being born and decided that as soon as Debra was ready, he'd have fifty kids if she wanted. He loved children and newborn babies. He didn't think that he'd deliver them; he'd be a nervous wreck if he were in that situation, but he would be there for Debra every step of the way.

After signing off on their birth certificates and

handing them in, he stayed in his office until things were settled in the waiting room. He didn't want to meet up with the parents of the couple and let the cat out of the bag about the babies. After they were told there were a lot of visitors to Millie's room, he didn't have the heart to tell them that only three visitors at a time. He let the staff handle it. They'd know the best way to make sure that Millie wasn't overwhelmed, nor would the babies.

As soon as he saw Debra, he felt the love for her that he did every time he saw her. She was his everything, and he could tell her that every minute of every day, and it still wouldn't be enough to let her know how deeply in love with her he was. They were on their way home at four in the morning, and all he wanted to do was sleep. With Debra. They'd work out the sex later.

Chapter 6

Debra was having fun finding a gift for Millie and her twins. She'd been told by one of the cashiers not to forget the older child, if there was one, or he'd be jealous of the girls. She'd already gotten him a few items for her basket and thought that she'd done well with him. As she was trying to decide on pink or purple for the girls, she got one in each color so that they could be twins but two different colors.

The little girls were identical twins. Just to look at them could tell her that, but Kahana had told her that there was a test that could be run and that told them everything they needed to know about the girls. She didn't remember what it was called, but was assured that they were identical in all ways. Debra thought that was the nicest gift to give them that they'd always have each other, no matter how big they got.

After shopping for the girls, she decided to head over to the hospital. Millie's family was going home tomorrow, having stayed an extra day to learn some things about caring for twins from the staff. She couldn't wait to have Kahana's child or children. She wanted to hold one of the babies so badly that her hands burned with the need.

The hospital was making it festive by having newborns in their nursery. You couldn't tell until you got to the nursery floor, but it was nice that they were so welcoming of the little ones. To think that if Millie and Charlie had left one day earlier, no one would have gotten to see the little girls here in town. There were so few births around here that they made a big deal out of every one of them.

The babies and Millie were asleep when she arrived. Her plan was to just peek at the babies and leave the gifts and leave. But Charlie was there with his son, who was sleeping, and he woke Millie up so that they could talk. She felt bad for the other woman; she knew how nice it was to have a nap.

Millie gushed over the outfits and loved that she'd thought to get pink and purple. She showed her the bracelets that she'd gotten too, with the knowledge that she could take them back if she didn't want to mark the girls with the little 'baby 1' and 'baby 2' bracelets. One was pink, the other was purple, like the sleepers that she'd gotten for the girls. Millie loved the idea as they'd used a marker and marked the bottom of their feet with their order of birth so they wouldn't mess them up.

"I was racking my brain trying to figure out a way to keep them straight. I know, as I get to know them, that I'll be able to tell them apart. I hope so anyway. But this will make it easier for everyone. Last night we used a magic marker on them to mark them with 'a' and 'b' so we could tell. It's also on their hospital bracelets, too." Debra told how there was a cashier at the store where she shopped who was an identical twin. She'd given her lots of advice. "Oh, good. I bet she said not to dress them alike. I hear that all the time from people. Even before I knew what I was having."

"She did tell me that it's nice to be able to express their selves when they get older. Apparently, they still dress alike when they go out. Different colors but the same outfit. And when they go home to their parents, they do dress alike for them. She said her fondest memories were when they were little, and people couldn't tell them apart. As you can imagine, they had fun with that as well." Millie laughed, and she decided that she liked them both a great deal. "I'm going to let you get back to your nap. I've heard all the stories about napping when the babies do. I do hope for you all the best when it comes to your growing family."

"Thank you, Debra, and I wish all the happiness for you and Kahana, too. He's a great man, but I doubt I have to tell you that. You must know him better than we do." She just grinned, her face heating up with what she took that to mean. "I'm sorry. I've embarrassed myself. You go on home now, and that'll be the end of our embarrassing stories. I can't believe I said that to you."

"It's all right. I knew what you meant." They hugged tightly, and just as she was leaving, Millie, a nurse came in with her lunch. She'd not realized how late it was when she looked at her phone and saw that it was nearly one in the afternoon. She was starving, too. Debra decided to see if Kahana was too busy to have lunch with her and called him on his phone. He answered with laughter in his voice.

"I was just thinking about you. What are you up to?" She told him where she was and what she was hoping to do. "Perfect. I just finished rounds and was headed to the cafeteria to have a bit of lunch myself. They're having baked potato soup today. One of my favorites they have here."

They met in the dining area and then ordered their food. She was having a salad with light dressing because the soup had too much sodium in it. She wasn't sure she'd like it anyway, as she didn't care for cheese in her soups. As soon as they sat down with their water and food, she decided that the salad was going to be perfect for her, as it had all kinds of greens in it that she loved.

"I just left Millie. She told me that they're going to be staying with his parents for a few days before they head back home. I think she wants to stay here as she's closer to his family than she is to her own." He said he'd caught that as well and wondered about it. "I didn't ask, but I have a feeling it has to do with the babies. I don't think they think that Charlie and Millie can raise twins on their own. She said her mother wants to move in with her as soon as she gets home to help out. I don't think that Millie will need help. She seems more than capable of raising three children on her own."

"That's just what I get when I'm around her, too. Especially the mother. She strikes me as someone who wants to take over. I don't believe that Millie will allow her to do that." Debra said that she didn't think she would either. "What did we get them as a gift so that I can be on the same page when they thank me for it?"

They both laughed at that, and she told him what she'd gotten. She even told him about the bracelets that she'd gotten for the little girls to tell them apart. Then she told him about the outfit that she'd gotten for Charlie, as well as the trucks that she'd gotten too. He'd been playing with them when she'd left the room.

"I have to go in tomorrow and release her. I could do it tonight and let her go home, but one more day of rest isn't going to hurt her at all." She told him how she was napping when she'd gotten there. "Yes, she is going to be good at taking advantage of them sleeping and napping when she can. I think that if anyone could handle having three kids in diapers at the same time, it will be her. Millie is a lot stronger than even she thinks that she is."

"You're talking about her mom." He nodded and looked around. That made her look around, too. "Are they here? The other couple? Are they here making trouble?"

"Not trouble, but asking questions about getting in-home care for her. And what she was going to need in the way of having a nanny for the babies. I don't think they ever mentioned they were going that way at all." She asked him what they might think of them staying with Charlie's parents for a few days. "I'm betting that didn't go over very well. She just seems like she needs to be in charge of everything. Like Charlie's grandma. Not as bad, but a great deal like her."

"That'll be bad. I'm betting that even Charlie will step in if it gets too difficult for Millie. I'd be so stressed out that I'd have to seek help in that area rather than raising three kids. Millie is a good mom, and she'll do a great job despite her mom." He agreed with her. "You're going to have to say something if she's going behind their back in getting help for them. Like I said, I don't think they're going to need it, but then I've never been a mom before. I'm excited about being one, but I'm not sure about babies."

"You ever babysit?" She said that she'd not, as it was too much for her mom to take her back and forth to the houses. "That's sad. I babysat, as did all my brothers. Mom said that there are no rules saying that a girl could only babysit children, and she got us out there in the world to do it. I really enjoyed it."

"I bet I would have too." She finished her salad and decided that she was too full for a dish of ice cream to go with it. Kahana had a dish of vanilla cream, and she enjoyed watching him eat it. She loved this man so much that she found that his having a simple dish of ice cream could be sexy. "I have some things that I have to do before I go home. Did you need me to do anything for you while I'm in town? I can pick up something for dinner tonight, too. It's the cook's night off, and I want to stay inside."

"I'm glad you said that because so do I. Pick up something easy and something that we can put on the grill. I'll do the cooking, and you can make us another salad." She asked him how grilled salmon sounded. "Perfect. Maybe a small baked potato, too. That would be perfection."

They talked for a bit more about nothing at all, and he had to go when he was paged. She made her way to the grocery store to pick up salmon for dinner and a couple of nice-sized potatoes. She was getting a bag of salad makings when she heard from Mac. She wanted to know if she and Kahana wanted to have dinner with them tomorrow night. Something on the grill.

"We're having salmon tonight if that helps you decide." She told her how she'd just got to see Millie and the new babies. "They're so beautiful with all that blonde hair, don't you think?"

"I do. I got to hold them when I was there this morning. They were having breakfast with Mommy. Charlie said that they nurse well too. It seems like they have the perfect family for them." She told her that she and Kahana had said the same thing. "I'm going to have a baby from hell who will never sleep through the night and want to nurse all the time. I'll be so worn out that I won't be able to keep Axel from finding a new woman."

"Now you're being silly. That man loves you so much right now that it's doubtful that he'd ever leave you." She said that Kahana loved her just as much. "I hope so. I can't imagine life without him around."

"I know just how you feel." They talked about some of the summer activities that were coming up around town, and she was happy that the Hathaways were involved in things that went on around their town. After setting up time to go to their home tomorrow night, the two of them closed the connection. She was

putting her cell phone away when it rang again. It was
the prison where Phil was staying.

"I need some money. I can't have any snacks at
all while I'm here, and I don't get enough for dinner."
She asked him why she should care about that. "I'm
only asking for some until I get my money from the
job they assigned me. After that, the job I have will put
money in my account. Just like fifty dollars is all I'm
asking for. I was going to ask for a hundred, but I knew
you'd say no to that."

"Damned right I would." She only thought
about it for a minute before telling him she'd do it. "I'll
set it up here in a little bit. I'm just coming home with
groceries, and they need to be put away."

"Thank you. Are you going to put in a hundred?
It will go a long way in making me have something to
eat when I want it." She told him fifty, and that was
all she was going to do. "I guess since you have all the
money, you're wanting to hang onto it. All right. I see
how—"

"Do you want the money or not? I don't care
either way." He told her that he was sorry and that,
yes, he wanted the money. "Good. If you said please
and thank you more often, I might want to help you
out. As it stands right now, you're on the line with
being nasty to me."

"I'm working on being a better person. They

have classes here that I can take that will help me with my anger issues. I didn't even know that I had them, and they said I've probably had them all my life." She told him that it was good that he was trying. "I noticed that you didn't disagree with me having anger issues. I'm assuming you knew I had them, too."

"You do, and working on them will go a long way for you when you get out of prison." He said that was another reason he was taking them because they would help him get a reduced sentence when his time for it was around. "Good for you. I wish you the best of luck. Now I have to get off here before my ice cream melts. I'll set it up when I get things squared away here."

After hanging up the phone, she did just what she said she was going to do. Getting things put away didn't take her all that long, and she was marinating the salmon a few minutes later. After getting that done, she got on the prison's website and set up the money for her cousin. She only put fifty into his account, then thought of how he'd been trying and decided to reward him for it. As she put in the hundred dollars that he wanted, she hoped that she wasn't making a mistake. He really was trying, and she wanted to show him that she'd been paying attention. As she was closing up the computer, she smiled to herself. It might not be bad having him around if he were going to act like he had some sense. She'd have to wait and see when he was out of prison. Which she hoped was going to be a long way in coming to an end.

~*~

Kahana was ready for a night at home. He also wanted to make love to Debra, but the two of them were exhausted from spending the night in the hospital when the twins were born. He thought that he could sleep standing up; he was that tired.

When Debra came into the living room where he was, she sat on his lap facing him. All thoughts of going to bed early were gone in that moment. He put his hands on her hips and held her still.

"I can control what happens if I'm like this." He could only nod. The thought of making any kind of sense with his words was gone. "I want to take you inside of me, and when I get too overwhelmed, I can stop."

"Yes, you can." He swallowed hard and looked up at her. "I can't be naked with you sitting on me this way. You'll have to stand up and undress too." There was only one thought in his head, and that was when she stopped because she had enough. Would he be able to as well? He hoped so. Love and trust were something that he couldn't hurt her with.

He hoped that he was making sense because, for the life of him, he didn't know what he was thinking about. The thoughts were just gone, but the words were there. He thought so anyway. What did he know? He was a desperate man on the brink of losing control. When she stood up, he did as well. Watching her undress, he nearly forgot what he'd been doing and sat back down. She looked at him as if he were some kind of idiot, and he couldn't help but feel that way as well.

"Aren't you getting undressed?" He nodded and stood up again. His legs were shaky, and his head was spinning. Getting undressed had never been this hard before. Pulling off his shirt and tie, he tossed them to the floor. After removing his belt, he realized that he was going to embarrass himself; he was so hard. Even as he pulled his pants off with his briefs and socks, he knew that whatever happened next was going to be the death of him. "If your phone rings, I'm going to destroy it. You told me you weren't on call tonight."

"No. I'm not." He sat back down on the couch when he was completely naked. "I'm sorry, love, but you're going to have to walk me through this. I'm not thinking all that well."

At her giggle, he smiled. They were going to be all right, he knew it. As soon as she sat back down on his lap, facing him, a calmness settled over him that he'd never known before. He was ready for whatever she wanted to do to him. He only hoped that he'd be able to survive to see the next morning.

Helping her settle over him, he held his cock in his hands until she was seated. Neither of them moved for several minutes. When she adjusted herself over him, just moving her hips just enough to have him hissing through his teeth, he held her still as she looked at him.

"I don't want to rush you, but you're killing me." Debra giggled again, and he thought that she was making fun of him. He didn't care right now as they were both naked and he was deep inside of her. Adjusting his own hips had her lying her head on his shoulder. "Are you all right?"

"I don't think so." He asked her what he could do for her. "I thought that I could control the situation, but I can't. I want you to lay me out on the couch and fuck me until I scream." She looked up at him. "I'm not even stressed about it. All I want to do is to come hard and scream my head off until you come."

"I can do that." She leaned into his mouth and kissed him. There was hunger there as well as a little bit of fear. He wouldn't hurt her for all the world, and he hoped that she knew that. "I want you too. We can do this. You just move the way you want, and I'll behave myself. At least I'll try my best to behave myself. I have the love of my life on my lap naked, and I couldn't be happier."

"You're filling me up." He moved again; this time, he couldn't have stopped if he wanted to. "I love the way that you feel deep inside of me. It's like you're a part of me and I want more of you."

"Let me adjust myself before I can't. My mind is working now, but it might not be in a few minutes." He moved just enough that he knew that he was deeper inside of her. When he reached up to pull her breast to his mouth, he pulled her hard nipple into his mouth and suckled hard. She moved on her own then, and he nearly went cross-eyed.

Debra moved slowly by canting her hips over him. When she moved back and forth, he held onto her hips to help her adjust to a rhythm. Kissing her, showing her how much he loved her, he held her tightly to him as he fucked her slowly. It was all he could do not to roll her to her back and take her hard. But this was all about her and not him. He knew that if he didn't come with her, he'd be all right, sore but all right, while she had her pleasure.

"I want to come." He told her that she could. "But I want you to come with me. I want to feel you when you come inside of me."

Rolling his own hips up to meet her downward stroke, he grabbed her ass and guided her over him. Every time she moved, he did as well until they had a good rhythm going. As she offered him her breast, he fed from it in short little nips that had her moaning and grinding him hard. He was loving every second of this. She was so wet that their sliding in and out was made slick by her cream.

When she stiffened above him, he held her through her climax. At her scream, he could only marvel at the beauty before him. Before he could think about her coming a second time, she was bowed back on his cock and holding onto his shoulders with her nails digging deep into his flesh. Christ, he thought, there is nothing more magnificent than a beautiful woman coming atop you.

When she came a third time, she laid her head on his shoulder until her body was calmer. He needed to take her, but was hesitant about how she was feeling. Almost as soon as he was ready to explode deep inside of her, his movements slow and steady, she told him to take her. He rolled her to the couch, taking her body hard.

"Fuck me." He would do whatever she wished, and when she screamed to him that she was coming again, he forgot about his own pleasure to watch her. He knew on some level that she was his, but this fucking was to claim her. To make her his. As soon as he gathered up her hands to put them above her head, he took her as hard as he could, with her matching each stroke with her own until they both came apart at the same time.

His breath stopped, his heart as well. Bowing back up and off of her, he knew that he was more than likely hurting her, but couldn't stop. He felt his cock empty, the pain of it so sudden that it took his breath away. When he came a second time, his painful balls filling again, he dropped atop of her and held her tightly, fearful that he was going to fly away if she so much as moved. At her giggling, some minutes later, he looked down at her with one eye open and asked her what was so funny.

"I don't think I have to worry about my heart giving out on me if we have a good fucking." He, caught off guard for just a moment, laughed too. "I feel fantastic."

"I feel like I'm crushing you. I need to move before we're stuck here this way forever." He tried to move off her, but the couch was just too narrow. Even as they worked to adjust themselves on the thing, he was careful of his cock. While he was sore right now, he knew that when he got up, he was going to pass out. Never in his life had he come twice in a row when he'd been having sex. She did that to him. And he loved her for it.

"I have to get up. My leg has a cramp in it." He moved that allowed her to stand up, but she nearly fell on him when she did. "I think I need you to rub it for me. It hurts."

After getting her leg to feel better, she laid down on the couch with him. They were spooned together with a blanket over them against the chill of the room. When he heard her soft snores, he closed his own eyes and drifted off. He didn't care if the house caught fire, and he was going to be naked outside; he was about as satisfied as he'd ever been in his life. And it was all due to the woman that he loved.

Waking up in the middle of the night, he realized that he was alone on the couch. Getting up, he grabbed his clothing and made his way to the stairs to the bedroom. Since her clothing was missing, he assumed that she'd gone on up to bed and left him there. He felt like he'd never slept so hard in his life. He felt that good.

Debra was in the bed when he entered the bedroom. Since there was a nightlight on in the room, he was able to see where he could lay his clothing and get into bed. He didn't know what time it was, but he was willing to bet that it was well after midnight. Crawling into bed with Debra, she curled around him and held him tightly. Closing his eyes, he was asleep in just a few seconds.

Getting up when the sun was shining in the room, he made his way to the bathroom and closed the door. He was sore all over his poor, abused body, and he thought that he'd do it again if given the opportunity. He hoped there would be plenty of those now that she was over her fear of hurting her heart again.

When he got back into bed after using the toilet, he was again wrapped up by Debra until he felt like he was home. Her hugs were wonderfully tight and full of love. As soon as he closed his eyes again, she spoke to him. He wasn't sure if she was sleep-talking or talking to him. He looked down at her when she asked him if he was all right again.

"I've never been better." She said that she was just as good. "Good. I would love to make love to you again while we're both naked and in bed, but I think you wore me out. So I'm just going to hold you in my arms until we either get up or go back to sleep."

"I'm all for sleeping again. I don't think I have the energy to move again." She put her head up under his chin. "I can hear your heart beating. It's so strong and steady. It's like you make me feel when I'm around you. I can take on the world, and love will make me triumphant. I love you so much, Kahana."

"And I love you." He dozed off and on but never really fell back to sleep. Once he got up the second time, leaving Debra in the bed, he took a long, hot shower and dressed in jeans and a t-shirt. There was nothing planned for the day, and since he wasn't going into the office, he decided that today was for them, and he was going to enjoy every second they had for each other.

When he made his way to the kitchen, Debra followed about thirty minutes later and was dressed as casually as he was. They made plans to have lunch in town after getting some things done around the house, then they'd go and get the last of the things they needed for the house.

"Your cousin left us set up nicely. The only things that we really need to replace are some of the towels that are in the master bathroom and a few more linens for the beds. Having only one set is fine because we have a washer and dryer, but I'd still like to have another set in case of an emergency." Debra agreed with him. "While we're out, I have to find me a shredder. I had one in my office when I was working for the firm, but I didn't think about one for my home office."

"I can just use yours then. If it gets to be too much, I can get me one as well." He said that his went to a firm that destroyed the files in them. "That might not be such a bad idea for my things as well. It's very sensitive stuff."

"What are you going to do as an attorney? I know you sold the firm, but what are your plans for your own license?" She told him that she might hang out her own shingle. "That would be great. That's what Axel is doing as well. You two should become partners. You'd be Hathaway and Hathaway."

Chapter 7

It didn't take her long to figure out that she couldn't work from her office at home. It was the one that her grandda had used, and it might have been all right for him, but not her. There were no windows to speak of. All his law books took up two entire walls that he kept in the dark side of the room. She hated the desk.

It was massive and heavy-looking, not for a woman of her size. The leather blotter had ink spilled on it in places, and the desk looked like it had been near a weedwhacker at some point, as the front and the legs of it were chewed up by something that did some serious damage to it.

The chair wasn't even a modern one. It didn't have wheels on it to slide up and under the desk. When she tried to lean back in it to take in the whole room, she nearly tossed herself out of it and across the room. Not to mention it was heavy and needed a new cushion in it, for the bottom was worn out. It was like she was sitting on stones, and they weren't particularly smooth either. The whole room needed a makeover. Kahana asked her what she was doing when he caught her standing on a chair trying to change a bulb in the overhead lighting.

"I don't even know where to begin in here. What do you think of when you come into this room?" He told her. "Oh well, I guess thinking about an old man would be about right. My grandda was in his nineties when he finally stopped taking cases. Phil said that was what killed him. That he could no longer go to the courthouse to try trials. I think he might be correct. I need to make this room look like a woman uses it."

"Rather than do it yourself, you should hire someone to do it for you. It might save you a lot of heartache later on." She asked him if he knew anyone who had an interior design degree. "My mom has one. She could probably have this room looking like a woman has always been here. I'm assuming that you're going to want to keep all the books that are in here."

"Yes, but they don't have to be in a dark corner of this room. I'd like to be able to use them. Having a collection this size is going to help me with cases all the time. He had newer volumes at his office in town. I'm having them cleaned and brought here. That's more than likely what I'm going to have to do to these."

"I'd talk to my mom. She more than likely will love to do this with you. I know her office—have you seen her office at home? It's beautiful. Very girly yet reflects my mom's taste very well. She has all these hidden things, too. Like, you don't see her filing cabinets because she has them hidden behind some kind of wall. I don't use her office, but she'd love to do yours if you asked her." She asked if he thought she'd be all right with doing a law office. "I don't know that an office for her clubs is all that much different than just a plain office. But you should ask her. I'm telling you, she'd love it. Have you given any thought to having your shingle put out with my brother? I know that I mentioned it just last night, but I'm betting he'd love that. I know that his building downtown has a second office in it already set up. He had it redone when he had the building refurbished."

"I thought you were joking." Kahana told her that he was sort of, but the more he thought about it, the more he liked the idea. "I'll talk to him. He might not want someone underfoot when he's working on cases. I would have to take on cases that I liked to do."

"I doubt he'd have a problem with that. He usually only works for the family on things and takes a case when something comes along that he thinks he might enjoy. He hated his other job so much that he was ready to quit being an attorney and find himself something else to do." She said that she wasn't even sure she had it in her to be on her own. "Then this would be perfect for the two of you. I know that you're going to finish the cases that your grandda had left on his desk. It would be the perfect place to have work done while your office is being updated. And it does need to be updated."

"I'll ask him if I can use his other office for a while and see what he has to say. We can work out later if I stay or not." Kahana said that sounded perfect. "That way, there's no pressure for him to think I'm going to be taking over his space. I would hate that myself."

"Did you want me to talk to him, or did you want to? I don't mind. But it won't be until tomorrow because I have to go to my office first. I have ten patients today, and I'm looking forward to it." She asked him how many he normally had. "Six if I was having a good day. But working up to more business is a lot harder than I thought it would be."

"I'll go and talk to him now. And your mom. I might as well get things rolling on my office so I can work in there. It's too dark and dank. I love the concept of having an office here, but that one would depress me too much." He said it would him as well. He wanted bright and airy. "I might have to have one of the walls redone to put in a couple of windows. I can't stand the thought of not being able to look outside on occasion. That would depress me even more than just the big, bulky furniture in there."

After Kahana left for his work, she gathered up her things and started to leave as well. But just as she was going out the door, she decided to take pictures of her office with the thought of it being something she could work with, even if Katie, the boys' mom, didn't want anything to do with helping her. It would be a big project to undertake, and she didn't know if the older Hathaway had time for that sort of thing.

She went to see Katie first. That way, she could tell Axel that she really was having work done on her office at home, and it would take a while. Katie was having a cup of tea with her husband, Benson, and they were having a good time. Debra almost hated to interrupt them while they were enjoying their time together.

"We were just talking about the twins and how much we're enjoying having babies around. With Mac pregnant now, it won't be long before we have little ones around of our own. Have you and Kahana talked about children?" She said that she and he were trying only because they both had demanding jobs. "I understand that. I had a job when I had the two oldest. I never worked so hard in my life, and that's when we decided I'd be better off at home with them rather than paying someone nearly all my check to watch over them. Best decision that I've ever made. What can I do for you?"

She explained to her about the office and how it was a man's place. After showing her the pictures of the room, Katie agreed that it needed a more womanly touch than it had now. Debra told her that she wasn't opposed to having a wall taken down to put in a few windows, either. She loved the bright sunshine when she was working. Then she asked if she'd help her with the project.

"Oh, I would love to do this for you. Yes, I can see changes now in my head." She started telling her about the desk that she needed, as well as how big the windows needed to be. "You need your own space that doesn't have tons of dust on it, too. What are you going to do in the meantime? I mean, while the office is being redone?"

"I'm going to ask Axel if I can use his extra space. Not as a partner, but just use it until I can either get myself a place on my own or just work from home. My grandda left a few cases on his desk when he died that I'm going to take care of. Plus, I can be helpful to the family as well." Katie said he was on his way over anyway for them to have a meeting about their wills. "Kahana and I need to change ours as well. My grandda was of the opinion that if it's been five years since you changed your will, it's time to get on it. Things can really change in that little bit of time."

"Oh, yes they can. We went from having two children when we first did ours to having six when we got around to it later. And some of the people that we had down as our children's godparents had passed away. It was just updated about ten years ago, and we thought that we should make another change." She said she was glad that things were getting updated for them. "I am as well. My sister left her things undone, and when she passed away, it was a nightmare to get things settled. I think there are still some things that aren't taken care of, but we did the best we could without a will. Everyone should have one, even if you don't think you own anything worth it. It's not going to leave the people you love scrambling around trying to figure out what to do with your stereo equipment. I know that's not quite right, but you understand what I mean."

"We have wealth, too, that needs to be dealt with if we pass. Even though we're both single, the two of us have a lot for someone to have to deal with." She asked when they were getting married. "Tomorrow afternoon. The judge said he'd come by and do it for us so that there is one less thing we have to worry about. Kahana and I both agreed that something at the courthouse was better than having a large wedding that no one will remember years from now."

Katie smiled. "I was hoping someday one of my boys would want a large wedding. It's been my dream to be the mother of the groom." They all laughed, and Debra told her she was sorry. "Oh, don't be. Axel and Kahana have always been the most practical of the boys. They wouldn't even allow me to have large birthday parties for them when they were little. It was too much fuss for them, they'd tell me. I did have more luck with the other four, but not by much. They didn't mind parties, but not with their friends. They just wanted family around, and that was all right too."

When Axel showed up, he brought flowers for his mom. He was the romantic of the boys, she told her, and she loved that about him. Kahana wasn't she was informed, and more than likely thought that having a big wedding would be a waste of money. Debra said she thought the same thing. Before they went to find themselves a place to spread out, she asked Axel about his office space.

"I've been thinking about you working there, too. I think we can get along all right." She said it would only be temporary as she was going to work from home. "No, you won't like that either. I mean, I work from home, but not a great deal. It's family time when I'm home, and you should do the same. I know that Kahana only devotes so many hours to his working from home so that he doesn't avoid the office. You can work with me on family projects, and we'll work our own cases when we have them. I'd love that."

"I think I would as well. I have enough law books to supply a large school. Grandda, even for as old as he was, bought the latest books when they were put up for sale. I have all his notes, too, on cases that he filed when he was a younger man, too. The firm is going to allow me to leave them there with the idea that they might use them sometime. I said that would be perfect." He said he might need to borrow from her as well. "I'm having my office redone at home. It's a mess. Not really a mess, but something that I've discovered that I can't work from. It was very masculine. Your mom is going to help me get it looking more like a woman works there than a bunch of old stogie men that didn't believe that women should do anything outside the home."

"He more than likely thought that he was right in that, too, from what I've heard about him. I take it all the partners are men at the firm." She said that they were going to take on more attorneys when they were finished buying the firm from her. "I thought that was a done deal. What's the hold up?"

"There are five partners in the firm, and a lot of underlings as grandda called them. They're going to make a few of them partners so that the cost to them all is a little less. I can wait on them. I'm still getting income from the cases that they're trying, so that's no big deal to me. I think when they finally get around to it, I'll make a bundle off the deal and be happy that I don't have to go to work there anymore. It wasn't a bad place, just very masculine." Axel told her that if she needed help, to let him know. He'd done this sort of buyout thing before and had a few ideas that she might want to incorporate into her dealings with them. "All right. I'll take you up on that."

The usage of the building that he was in was finalized, and he said that they'd get around to what the rent was going to be sometime. He said he wasn't in any kind of hurry as he was happy to be working for himself. She was, too, she told him, and was glad that they'd be able to work things out. She was on her way home again when the others went to the office to update their will. Debra was excited for this next phase of her life.

The first thing she did when she got home was to call someone to come and pack up the office. Then it was to send the books off to be cleaned and restored if needed. Grandda took great care of his books, so she didn't see any problem with them being in bad shape, but wanted to make sure. There was a lot of money in law books, and the value of them rarely went down.

~*~

Kahana loved being busy. It made the time go by faster, and his workload seemed less of a burden on his time. Also, he was able to be there for someone who might not have had a doctor yet. He even got to generate some more business when some of the people said that they were going to tell their family members about him.

"We have a walk-in who would like to talk to you about something. I couldn't get anything more out of her than that." He asked how old she was. "I would say she's about sixteen, but I can't tell anymore. They all look like they should be in high school to me."

"I get that too." He asked when he was going to see her. "I mean, did we have to squeeze her in? I don't mind at all. I was just thinking I like being busy."

"She's your next appointment. If you can get her to fill out some of the paperwork that I gave her, that would be great too." Margaret was his assistant and bookkeeper. They got along well, and he was happy to have her on board. "Just be sure that you want to take her on. I'm worried about her being pregnant or something. And she's too young for that, no matter what I think her age might be."

"All right. You should come in with me." She said she had the phone to man and that she couldn't do it. "I guess you were right. I need to hire a couple of nurses. While I like being able to spend time with patients, I'm going to stretch myself too thin, and that won't bode well for me."

"I'm forever right. You have to get that into your thick head." They both laughed at her joke, and then she got serious. "I'll put out an ad in the morning for a couple of nurses. Even if they want to work part-time, it will be better than nothing. I can't be in two places at one time, and you need the help. Especially when things start to pick up the way that they are."

"All right. If you happen to have a few minutes, just drop into the room. I don't know what's going on, but I'd like to not be arrested for anything while my business is picking up." Margaret said she'd do her best, and that was all he could have hoped for. "Just be around if things get wonky. I really don't want to go to jail when I'm getting married tomorrow afternoon."

The woman, there was no doubt that she was older than she looked to even him, told him her name was Sarah MacMillen and that she was twenty-four years old. She also said that she wanted to get on birth control because she'd met this guy who she wanted to get intimate with, and she didn't want to have a baby. Ever.

"I can do that for you. However, it would have to be after an exam. I can't just put you on birth control without making sure you're healthy enough to be on them. There are side effects, too, that I'd like to discuss with you as well." She said that would be all right as she'd been reading things on the internet about her options. "Good for you. That's really smart. There is also the fact that the only sure way to not get pregnant is to not have sex. I'm not telling you not to be intimate with this person, but you have to realize that even condoms aren't a hundred percent. They break too."

"I understand." She seemed to have her facts all lined up for him to go over, and he was proud to help her. More people should be prepared when they go to see the doctor, and they'd be better informed when the time comes. "I know too that I have to be on them for a few months to make sure that they're taking effect. I'm not saying I want to jump into bed with him as soon as I take the first pill, but I know that I will still need to be careful. I don't want to have children at all."

"I can understand that as well. It's your body and your timeline." She thanked him for telling her that instead of telling her she might change her mind later. "You might, but that will be totally up to you. Don't let anyone pressure you into anything that you don't want to do. As I said, it's your body, and you are the one to decide if you want to have children or not."

After talking to her for a few more minutes, she decided to set up a time for him to do an exam. In the meantime, he ordered blood work for her to have done, which would give him a heads up if there was anything wrong. He was happy to be able to help her with her needs and was glad that she was willing to give him a chance to be her new doctor.

After she left, filling out the paperwork that Margaret needed. The file was set up for her, and she was ready to go as his new patient. He was sort of excited to know that he was going to be helping someone who needed not just a doctor but advice as well. He was glad that he'd had the time to spend with her, too. At the other firm he worked for, they only allotted twenty minutes with each patient because they couldn't make any money if they spent a lot of time with one person. That was the one thing that he had hated the most about the other place. He didn't have time to get to know anyone there that he treated.

For the rest of the afternoon, he saw his patients and spent as much time with them as he could. As the day was winding down, he could feel the pressure behind his eyes that made him wish that he'd slept better last night. Not that he would give up making love to Debra, but it was wearing him to the bone to be up late and get up early.

"Last patient. It's Mrs. Booth. She wants to talk to you about the twins and they're sleeping habits." He asked what that might mean. "She said that she's having trouble getting them to sleep at the same time. She wondered if you had any advice. She also mentioned that she thinks that they're not getting enough from her breastfeeding. I think I'll leave that one up to you."

"Thanks." He went to the room she was in and could see right away that she wasn't sleeping well.

There were bags under her eyes, and she looked like she could cry at any moment. He asked her what was wrong, and she burst into tears. "Oh, honey, it's going to be all right. I got you."

"They are starving to death, and I'm dying trying to keep up with them. I just don't have enough milk coming in for them, and I'm worried that someone is going to take them from me because I'm a shitty mom. I don't want that to happen. I love them so much that it hurts to think that my parents are going to be taking them away from me because I don't know what I'm doing."

"I'm sure we can figure things out. Where are they now?" She said they were with Charlie, and he was dealing with them so that she could have a walk. "And you walked to here, I'm assuming. I'm sure that it's not as bad as you think it is. Have Charlie bring them in, and we'll go from there. I'll weigh them both and figure out a supplement that you can give them when you just don't have enough milk coming in."

"They'll take them away from me if I give them formula." He asked her who. "My parents. They have it in their head that I'm going to be a terrible parent to them, and they're going to try to take them from me. And giving them formula will be just the ammo they need to take them. I love them, Kahana. I can't just sit by while they take them from me."

"I'll call Axel. I'll see what he has to say about them trying to take the girls away from you. This is just stupid. Don't they realize how much stress they're putting you under by threatening you like this?" She said they wouldn't care; it would just be one more thing to add to their list of how she's failing as a mom. "There will be no more talk about how you're failing as a mom. You're a good mom, or you wouldn't be here right now trying to figure things out. I'll call and see what he can do. Or better yet, I'll call my wife. I sometimes forget that she's an attorney too. We'll get this figured out. In the meantime, call Charlie and have him bring in the girls. Charles too. We might as well make sure that they're all healthy."

While Debra was talking to the parents, he examined the kids. They were all doing well, and the twins' weight was right on target. But if she wasn't sleeping because they were nursing all the time, he thought it was a good time for her to introduce formula to them. Just at night for their last feeding, and it would give her a few hours of uninterrupted sleep. At least he hoped so.

Charles seemed to like his little sisters, but he was worried about his mom. She was crying all the time, and it worried him. People should watch what they say around little ones; they had stress too from their cruel words.

After talking to Charlie and Milly, he thought that they were in a better frame of mind. Charlie said he wasn't worried about her parents, but from what Debra said to them, he might should be. They were dangerous, and if they got the kids, they had enough money to get them out of the state. That would be bad for them when caught, too.

"I think if I could just get one night's sleep a week, I'd feel better. But when one is asleep, the other is awake and hungry. I knew that raising twins was hard, but I didn't have time to prepare myself for this. I need to get some sleep." Debra spoke up then. She said that she'd help with the twins tonight, and she could get some sleep. "I don't want to do that to you. I'm exhausted, and I'm getting used to them. You've never had children before. No offense.

"None taken. I can watch them for a few hours. Charlie can take a shift, and so can the rest of the Hathaways. You look terrible, and if your parents could see you now, they'd think that you weren't getting any rest at all. Just let us do this for you for a couple of nights. You'll feel better, we'll all feel better knowing that we're helping you out." She said that she couldn't ask them to do that. "No one was asking. I'm telling you that you need to get some sleep before you have to deal with your parents. We can help you get a good night's sleep or a couple of them and take over the care of the little ones. Even Charlie will help. I'm betting right now he's agreeing with us in that you need your rest, too. It wouldn't be that bad."

In the end, it was settled, and she would go home and take a nap. The children would all come to his house, and they'd hang out with them for a while. Once Charlie and Dani found out about Milly's parents and the children, she went to make sure that Milly laid down and took a nap.

"I had no idea this was going on. I mean, I could see that she wasn't getting any good rest, but I figured that if she needed any help, she'd ask for it." Kahana explained about her parents and what she was afraid they'd do if they found out that she was giving the children formula instead of breast milk. "Oh, pea shaw. She had twins that she didn't know about. I think she's doing a fantastic job of raising them without any prep work. Why, we had to go out and buy them another crib; they were so unprepared for them both. She'll get some rest now, even if I have to get up in the middle of the night and make her."

He knew that was what would happen. They were good families, and they would do it without asking. Milly was so exhausted when he took her home that she fell asleep in his car. He wondered why she'd let it go for so long and not ask for help. He couldn't wait to meet her parents. They sounded like a bunch of ass holes. Well, now that everyone was involved, things wouldn't go the way that they had hoped. Who would threaten a new mom about taking her children away just because she had to give them formula? He supposed there were people who only believed in nature's own way, but there were circumstances where things were just out of their hands that they couldn't just breastfeed.

After getting her settled in and her mother-in-law watching over her, he made his way back to the office. He knew that there were going to be some rules made, and he couldn't wait to hear what they were. His family was involved now with the Booths, and they'd make sure that things went well, or he'd sic Mac onto them. That would be the best way to deal with them, having Charlie's little sister pounce on them. That would be funny.

Chapter 8

Yolanda couldn't understand why she couldn't see her granddaughters. They were all staying with the Booths instead of her home, but she could handle that since her daughter had just had them, and there would be the mess to keep up with. But that didn't mean she couldn't see what she was doing to the children. They were her grandkids, too, weren't they?

Of course, her house was miles away from anyone. They had purposely built themselves a home out from town so that they'd have the privacy that they desired. As it was now, it was over an hour from their home to the hospital and even more to the Booths' home on the other side of town. That's why she didn't visit her daughter any more than she did. It was just too much work to go that far when it was just to see the girls for a few minutes.

"Why can't we see them more than a few minutes at a time, Daddy? I'm betting that the Booths get to hold them all the time. If we were to get them, then we'd have them as much as we want." He told her again that he didn't want to raise twin girls, he was finished with being the one who raised children, as his were all grown up. "She's not going to do a good job of raising them. Remember how she was when she was a child? Forever into something that caused us trouble. I won't have her embarrassing me again."

"For God's sake, Yoland, she's nearly thirty years old. She's a damn sight better mother than she would have been at six. And she's done all right with that boy. Though why they named him after his father is something I don't like. Should have named it a good solid name like Wilbur. But that's water under the bridge. I'm not going to help you with those girls if you manage to get them from our daughter. Not that I think you can, but you won't be bringing them here to mess with my quiet time. Do you hear me?"

"We'll hire nannies to help out. We won't even know they're around until we want to see them. I just don't like that she's had them two little girls and we're not there to help her raise them. She should have come here so that we could have taken over their care and taken them from her." He just stared at her. "Well, I'm going to try and see what sort of things she's doing as their mother so that I can get the courts to take them from her."

"You do that, and she'll never speak to you again. You heard what she said at the hospital about those girls. They were hers, and she wasn't going to have you fooling around in their lives like you tried to do with Charles." He stared at her before speaking again. "I don't want a bunch of kids running around here, Yolanda. If you so much as try to bring them into the house, I'll divorce you so quickly you won't know what happened. And you signed a prenup. If you try me, you'll be raising those girls all on your own. What's a sixty-six-year-old woman without a home or money going to do with two infants and a toddler at their feet? I'm telling you right now, just leave well enough alone." He snorted, but before she could tell him that was a nasty way to speak, he spoke to her again. "I'm going to tell her what you're up to. So she can be prepared. And I'll help her, too, to keep you from taking those girls. I won't have it. Not one bit."

"You wouldn't dare." He told her to try him. "Daddy, what if she tries to keep them from us? What will you do then?"

"What you're doing is a sure-fire way of her keeping them away from us because you'll be in prison. And they'll know for sure that I knew because you don't make a move without telling me what's going on. Not that I have to agree with you, but I'd know what you're doing. Don't do it. I can't make myself any clearer than that. You do this, and you'll be on your own and without my support. I hate to threaten you, Yolanda, but I swear to you that if you try this, I'm going to move heaven and earth to have you arrested.

You no more need to be raising those kids than I do being called a daddy at my age. People already look at me oddly enough when you call me that. My name is Wilbur, not Daddy. Your daddy died more years ago than he'd been living."

"Dad…Wilbur, they're your grandkids too, you know. Why can't we raise them like they need to be raised? I know that there are rules that are supposed to be in place about babies anymore, but I raised her to be a good person; I can do it again." He asked her if she was going to be changing shitty diapers again. "Get real. I never changed them when Millie was little. What do you think nannies are for? No, I'll take them from her because she's going to be a terrible mom, and the two of us will be happier for having them around us. Children make you feel younger; I've always heard that."

"You're not going to get the chance to see if that's true or not because as soon as I can get to a phone, I'm going to tell her what you're up to. I swear to you that I'm going to do it. I might even hire her a lawyer so that she can win the case against you." He shook his head. "You might be able to get around me with getting them, and that would be on you. But the moment that you try to set foot into this house, I'm going to kick you to the curb. I'm not kidding you, Yolanda. I will turn you out of this house so fast you won't know what happened to you."

"Why would you do that to me when I've given you nearly fifty years of marriage? I've been a good wife, too." He said that she had until she started talking nonsense about raising babies at their age. And he wasn't going to have it. "You say that now, but as soon as one of them snuggles up to you, you'll change your mind."

"There will be no chance of them snuggling up to me because as soon as you leave here to do this, I'm going to call the police. You'll not get out the door without—how are you going to get them? Just grab up three children in your arms while your daughter is screaming her head off at you to stop? How are you planning on getting from there to here? I'm going to make it so you can't take a car anywhere. Which brings me to this. There won't be any nannies. If you want to raise them, then by god you'll do it on your own. No help, no money, no house. If you think I'm kidding you about this, you walk right on out of here and try it. In fact, I'm going to call my daughter now and let her know what you're planning. That should nip it in the bud as far as you're concerned."

"If you don't help me, then I won't speak to you anymore." He asked her if she was making a promise, one she couldn't keep. "I'll leave you then. What would all your friends say if you were to suddenly be without a wife?"

"They'd ask me what took me so long to get rid of you is what they'd ask." She didn't care for his answer and told him so. "I don't care, Yolanda. I really don't. You can't raise them babies any better than our Millie can, and that's the truth. You'll be into so much of a mess with her that she'll never have another thing to do with you. And I'll get to see the babies even if I have to sneak around to do it. I won't allow what you're doing to ruin my relationship with my grandbabies. And especially not my daughter and her husband. I like Charlie. He's a good man and has worked hard all his life. If you do this, and I'm not telling you again, I will not help you. You'll be completely on your own if you try. And trying will be the same as doing, as far as Millie will be concerned, and she won't have another thing to do with you."

"You do whatever you think you have to do, but I'm taking those children away from her. She's not been a good mom to Charles, and she won't be to those girls either. You just wait and see that I'm right." He just picked up his newspaper. "I'm telling you right now, Daddy. If I can't have those babies to raise on my own, then there will be hell to pay by you and Millie. She no more deserves them than I need to be treated the way you're treating me right now."

"No." That was all he said, and she was about

as pissed off at him as she'd ever been. How did he get to choose what she did or didn't do just because she signed a prenup when they married? Damned man. She was going to do it to spite him if she had to. He'd see she was right as soon as they were all in her house together. And Millie would understand too. She knew she couldn't raise those three little ones on her own. It would take her to show her how she was messing up all the time.

Yolanda decided that she was going to go and see her daughter and the babies first thing in the morning. Spend the day with them to get the lay of the land, so to speak. She'd record in her notebook every misdeed that her daughter did while raising the girls. It wouldn't be that hard. Millie had always been a scatterbrain when she'd been little, and she didn't believe that she was any different than she was right now. While she liked Charlie too, he was a bendable man, and she'd have him agreeing with her in no time. Then Daddy would see. She would be a good mom to all three of them, and Charlie and Millie would be just fine without anyone to raise.

"Mr. Stanford, you have a phone call." He never cared who it was from, but would get up and leave her to answer the phone in mid-conversation. It annoyed the piss right out of her when he did that. "Would you like to take it in the library, sir?"

"Yes, that'll be fine. And could you please bring me a cup of tea, April? You know the kind that I like. And a couple of cookies before dinner would be great too."

Something else that Daddy did was say please and thank you to the help. She'd never once done it and wouldn't. They worked for them, and that should be payment enough for them. It wasn't as if she were a snob or anything, but the very reason that you had servants in the first place was so that you could order them around. Sitting in her chair, the staff knew better than to ask her if she wanted tea as well. If she didn't ask for it, then she didn't want it. She had a little game that she played with them. As soon as she got her husband's tea, then five minutes later she'd ask for one too. It would get her every time when they had to make two trips out of the kitchen to bring them tea.

She thought about going to see her daughter tonight, but she didn't want to be up late getting home. The babies would be cranky in the evening hours, she remembered how bad her daughter was when she would be with the nanny so late in the evening. She didn't want anything to do with her during those hours, and they made sure that she didn't have to.

It didn't bother her that Millie had been raised by nannies. She would have had more children had she been a better baby to them all. But alas, Millie had been a bad child, and it only stood to reason that she'd be a rotten person too. She was forever wanting a good and dutiful daughter, but she got Millie instead. So long as she could raise the twins like good people, then she didn't really care if her daughter ever spoke to her again. Yoland knew she was a good mother, and she proved it by having Millie as a daughter. No matter how bad she'd been, she didn't get rid of her when she could have. That had to say something about her character, didn't it?

When Daddy didn't come back from the office in a goodly time, she decided that she was going to show him and go up to bed without him. The two of them didn't share a room anymore and had since become strangers to their nighttime habits. She liked her privacy, and he liked his quiet time. They both got what they wanted, and there was no one around to tell them they were doing it all wrong.

Going up to bed also allowed her to be able to get up early in the morning and surprise her daughter. That would be the perfect time to get all the good dirt on her about her mothering skills. Or the lack of it. The house would be a mess, and there wouldn't be—she forgot they were staying with the Booths. She wondered how much of a mess they were having since her daughter was living with them. No doubt they'd be ready to get rid of the family, too. Perfect timing, she thought, to get in and get the kids before anyone was the wiser. The Booths would more than likely help her out with them just to get them out of their hair.

She'd be in and out, and no one would care but Millie. She might fuss for a bit, but once she got used to not having them around all the time, she'd come around, too. Yolanda thought it would be wonderful to have the children around all the time. It would be like she said, they'd make them younger. Tomorrow, before she left, she was going to have to call a service to have nannies brought to their home. There was no reason to wait until they were there before calling in help. And she wanted all the help she could get once they were in the house. Daddy wouldn't even mind once he realized that this is what she wanted. He didn't usually give in to her demands on things. However, this would be different. He'd benefit from it as well.

~*~

Millie hung up the phone and looked at her husband. Her dad had called her, and she couldn't believe the things that he'd just told her. Having it on speaker phone so that Debra and Charlie could hear didn't even make it seem more real. It was as if everything in her life had been pulled out from under her in a second.

"She's not going to get your kids." Millie nodded at Debra, but she was distracted. "Millie, listen to me. She's not going to be able to get your kids from you. No court in the land will give a sixty-something-year-old woman three children who will be out of a house and money for any reason. She's going to jail if she even tries to take them. You heard what your dad said, he was going to divorce her in the morning for her talk."

"I don't understand why she thinks she knows anything about me. I was raised by the nannies of the house. Then, when I turned thirteen, she sent me off to boarding school. I was nineteen years old when I came home once, and that was only to see my dad. She never visited me once, but Dad did all the time." Millie didn't know what to think about her mother's plot to take her children away and raise them on her own. "What does she think she's going to do? Have them raised by more nannies so that she can pretend to be their mother? I'm their mother, and I can raise them the way that I see fit."

"Good for you. You got this. And your dad said that she's going to be coming by soon and try to take them when you're not looking. I don't know how that's possible, but I've dealt with people who think things like this all the time. They just don't understand when they're wrong." Millie was glad that she'd gotten help when she did, or she might well have been able to call her an unfit mother. The first night home with Dani there to help her, she'd slept nearly fourteen hours straight through, and the kids were doing great. "They seem to like the formula and are more rested than they were before. I know that I am."

"You're on a good routine now, and they can feel that you're less stressed. Isn't that what Kahana said? They can feel when you're stressed, and it stresses them out. I can understand that. When I had my heart attack, I was stressing out everyone around me." Millie looked in the two cribs that held her infants. And Charles was on the bed with her, reading a book with his father, when her dad called. Things were much better than they were even five days ago. Then her dad called her to warn her about her mother. "Weren't you going home tomorrow?"

"I was. Should I now? I'd rather be here than at home by myself with her coming around." Her in-laws came into the room after Charlie had gone to get them. After telling them everything that was going on, they said she'd be better off staying here with them because there was no way she was going to get out of the house with the babies. "I don't want to bring her madness down on you guys. And that's all I can think that it is. Madness. Why would she want to take my babies away from me? I'm a great mom now that I have a routine going on. She can't be serious about this is all I can think about."

"There isn't any point in taking any chances.

We'll keep an eye on her the entire time she's around. She won't get by us." Dani took one of the babies when she started to fuss and rocked her as she continued. "She tries to take my grandbabies from this house, and there will be hell to pay. I'm not kidding either. I'll have her arrested so fast that she'll be in jail before she realizes that what she did was stupid."

Millie had to laugh. They were all so good to her. Even when she needed to be down for a few days, everything catching up with her, Dani had treated her like her daughter rather than a daughter-in-law. It was a good feeling being loved by strangers more than she had been by her mom her entire life. But her dad was a good man.

"He said that he was going to talk to his attorney tomorrow to start the divorce proceedings. He knew it was going to come to this as soon as I told them that I was going to have another baby." Her dad seemed to be resigned to the fact that she was going to try to take the children from her. He also told her that he had nothing to do with it and wouldn't. He was too old to raise children again, and while he loved her to pieces, he didn't want to raise her three kids when he had his golden years ahead of him. But he would hire an attorney for her if she needed to have one. "I told him that I had hired you, Debra. I hope that's all right. I think before this is all finished, I'm going to need someone to be in my corner instead of my mother. Christ, I can't believe that she's doing this to us. It's like something out of a nightmare."

It took them the rest of the evening to get things worked out. She was going to stay with the Booths for a few more days until they could get the locks changed on her home so that she couldn't just come in. She'd given her a key when they first bought the house, never thinking it would be a terrible idea. Now that the locks were going to be changed, she thought that she should do a few more things, like hire a nanny for nighttime.

Kahana said that she wasn't a bad mother because she needed help. She was a smart woman and knew that she couldn't do it on her own. And raising three children under the age of five was hard enough on the strongest of people. And unlike some people, they could afford it.

Also, she was going to make sure that, if nothing else, every day she was going to get herself up and cleaned up before starting her day. It was the least she could do for herself that made her feel good. Even if she only got to brush her teeth, she was going to do something for herself daily so she'd feel better than she did a few days ago.

At seven the next morning, her dad called to see if he could come by and have breakfast with her. Since she was just getting in the shower, she told him that it would be wonderful. As soon as he arrived at seven-thirty, not only was she dressed for the day, but she'd put on a bit of makeup and done her hair. She felt positively wonderful. Charlie commented on her beauty as they were sitting down to breakfast with the Booths.

"My goodness, child. You looked beautiful. Who would know you've just given birth two weeks ago? If your mother could see you now…well, she'd not have anything nice to say to you, that's for sure. But that's her loss." After kissing her dad on the cheek, he joined them for their first meal of the day. She loved this time of the morning. The girls were fed and cleaned up, and Charles was playing with his blocks. It was quiet in the house as well. Something that she loved more than anything. "I think that she's coming to see you today. She was up when I left, and that never bodes well for people. I don't know what her plans are for the day, but I'd expect her soon. She's on the warpath, and I'm going to avoid her for the rest of the week if I can."

"I don't blame you, Wilbur. I'd stay clear of her, too, if I could." Charlie sat down next to her and kissed her on the cheek. "Doesn't she look beautiful? I can't believe how lucky I am to have such a beautiful wife."

They mostly talked about her mom and what she might be up to. At eight, not only did her mother show up, but she had the police with her. She said she was here to take her children back. All hell was about to break loose, and she wasn't sure how to handle it right now. She did the only thing that she could and called the Hathaways. Debra was her lawyer, and Axel was going to help her with the trial. Because as surely as she was sitting here, she was going to press charges against her mother.

"What are you doing here? I thought you were going to the club or something." Mom looked at Dad when he didn't answer her. "Nothing to say? I told you I was going to do this, and you should have listened to me. I want to raise the children right, and there is no way that you're going to keep me from doing so."

"Isn't there? I filed for divorce this morning before coming here to have breakfast with my family." She called him a liar. "Believe what you wish, but it's a done deal. I told you that if you went through with this, I was going to do it. Now that you have, the locks have been changed on the house, and your accounts have been closed as of seven-thirty. You're broke. And homeless to boot."

"You can't leave me out in the cold. I have three of our grandbabies to raise. What will your friends say when they find out that you divorced me rather than seeing that your grandbabies are raised well?" He told her what he said he'd told her yesterday, they'd wonder why it took him so long. "I will not allow you to do this to me, Daddy. I'm going to go back to the house with my children, and you're not going to do a thing about it."

"My name is Wilbur. I have been telling you that for so long that I'm sure that the furniture knows my name. I haven't ever been your daddy ever, and I don't like you calling me that anymore. It's Wilbur Stanford." Her dad stood up and asked her mom to leave. "We were having a nice breakfast until you came here. Whatever are the police for? I'm sure they have things to do that are more important than an old woman trying to kidnap babies from their parents."

"How dare you?" Mom turned and looked at her. "Where are *my* children? I want to show these people how you treat them like you did things when you were a child."

She didn't so much as look in the living room where they were sleeping in their cribs. Even Charles was playing quietly while in the same room with them. As soon as her mom turned on her heel and headed toward them, she grabbed Charles by the arm and jerked him up from the floor. Standing in front of the cribs, she told the police to get the babies as she was leaving with them right now.

"You're hurting my arm." The slap to Charles' face was so sudden that she didn't react at first. Before she could get to her son and comfort him, her mother was flipping over the back of the couch and onto the floor between the two cribs. No one said a word until Charles came to her. "Mommy, she hit me in the face. And she hurt my arm."

"I'll make sure you're all right. Uncle Kahana will have a look at you, and he'll make sure you're not hurt." Millie looked at her husband when he asked if they were all right. "Did you hit her?"

"I did, and I'd do it again if she tries to hurt one of mine." He turned to the police and said he was pressing charges against Yolanda for abuse of his son. And for attempting to kidnap his daughters. "I want her out of this house now and in jail before I call my attorney. You'll do that for me, won't you?"

"Yes, sir. When we came here, we didn't know what to expect. She said that you were abusing your children in a sexual way. Not that we believed her, but we had to come with her to see. We had no idea that she was going to hurt anyone. We even called special services to take the children away if necessary. I can see that it was all in her head." Charlie said that was right, and her dad vouched for him. "We'll take her in now. I would imagine that she's been planning this for some time. She had notes on the things that you were both doing to your children while you were living here."

"Whatever she said is untrue, officers. She came here to kidnap my children and hurt one of them. I want to press charges against her, and I'll be downtown as soon as I'm finished having my breakfast." The officer said he could see that. As soon as she came around, Mom was put in the back of a cruiser and taken away. "Dad, are you really going to divorce her over this?"

"It's been a long time coming, and I'm glad that she's shown herself to be a nutball with others around. She's been driving me crazy for the last twenty years, but with these children, I just don't know what to think. She had it in her head that she was going to raise them better than you could. I don't know how that was possible. She never had a thing to do with you when you were a child. And just look at you with your babies right here. I couldn't have been more proud than I am of Charlie. Damn, but I wish I could have been the one to hit her. You did a good thing in protecting your family, young man, and I am happy to call you son."

The breakfast was a good time, and they all had their fill. Dad got to hold the babies, and she thought he looked his happiest doing it. As soon as he left, too, telling them that he had his will to change, they all decided to go into town and have a morning of it. There were charges to press, too, and she was looking forward to her mom being in jail for a while. It would certainly be something that she could live with, her not being around much.

Chapter 9

Kahana felt bad for little Charles. His arm was broken from being snapped up from the floor, and he didn't know who was more upset, his dad or his mom. Charles thought it was cool to have a rainbow cast on his arm, and after the pain medication was given to him, he was all right with that, too. The kid was feeling pretty good when he left the office, and he couldn't have been happier for the three of them.

"Do you suppose she would have treated them all that way, given the chance? I was just wondering because of the way she hurt that little boy without anything being said to him." Kahana told Debra that he thought she had been abusive all their lives, and it was just catching up to her. "I'm so glad that we were able to help them out. Did you hear that they're going to be moving in with her dad? I guess he's leaving the house to the two of them so that they can bring joy into the house again. I wonder if there was any joy in that house with her there."

"Doubtful. Wilbur isn't the least bit surprised that she hit Charles. He said that he wished he'd have warned them sooner of her tendencies to lash out at people." He told Debra how she'd hit a couple of the staff, too, and they had to be compensated in order not to press charges. "I find it sad that Wilbur waited so long to divorce her. I think he's been unhappy for years, but just put up with her. I hope he gets the life that he wants from now on. I don't know that she'll face much jail time with this, but he'll have everything set up so that she's out of his life from now on while she's in jail."

"I feel the most sorry for Millie. To have her life turned upside down like it is just because her mother decided that she was going to take her children from her. How sick do you have to be to think that you could do a better job at raising three kids when all you have is the clothing on your back? I heard that he did warn her several times that if she went through with this, he was going to divorce her. I think that he'll be a happier man from now on."

"I agree with you." Debra said that she had to get home as she had things to take care of. Kahana hated to see her go, but he had other patients to see to himself. As soon as she left, he got down to work so that he could get out on time today. He had a wife at home that needed him, and he wasn't going to shirk on his duties at this point in the game. Kahana was smiling when he saw his next patient.

His day went well. He didn't have anything go

wrong today, so that was a plus. Tomorrow, he had rounds to make at the hospital, and he was looking forward to that. Then back to work at his new place, where he was seeing more and more patients all the time. He'd been told that word had gotten out how good he was, and people liked that he was local. Kahana liked being busy, and with all this coming his way, he was staying busier daily.

"Hey, doc." He was seeing the Anderson boy, who had broken his leg while playing around the gym equipment at the local gym. He'd been trying to make the treadmill go as fast as he could, and he'd slipped and fell. His parents were having a fit over the fact that no one was watching him. Kahana stayed out of it. "Mom said that I can have a boot soon. Does that mean I'll be able to gimp around?"

"You won't be getting a boot anytime soon. You have two broken bones in your leg that have yet to have time to heal. You need to stay off your leg before you hurt yourself more." He told him that he was bored. "Bored or not, you're never going to heal right if you keep getting up on your cast while you're healing. If you don't behave with it, I'll have Doctor Martin put you back in the hospital, and we'll see where that gets you."

"The hospital is the worst. The three days I was in there, I thought for sure my head was going to pop off. The nurses are mean too." He just stared at him. "Okay, they're not mean, but they have a lot of rules to follow, and I don't think they liked me all that much."

"Because you weren't doing as you were told." He examined the sprain to his wrist and decided that it was finally healing the way that it should have been. "I can put a smaller cast on your wrist, but if you bang it up again, I'm going to have you put in a cast from your fingers to your shoulder, and we'll see how you like that. I'm not kidding you right now, Todd. You have to settle down before you hurt yourself more."

"I wish I hadn't of tried to make the treadmill work faster now." He was sure that everyone wished that for him. He was much too much of a boy to try to settle down. Then he thought that perhaps a girl might be just as hard to keep from hurting herself, so he didn't voice that to him either. "Mom is going crazy with me being home all the time. She tries to keep me down, but I have to outsmart her sometimes. It's boring lying on the couch when there's nothing to do. Mom said I should do my homework, but that ain't no fun either."

Oh, how he wanted to tell the boy that if he'd been doing what he was supposed to be doing, none of this would have happened, but he didn't. It must have been hard on his mom taking care that he didn't get up, and around all day, he didn't want her mad at him, too. As soon as he was fitted for a wrist brace instead of the cast he had on, Kahana knew that he was going to be back in here with it hurting again. There was no settling the boy down so he could heal.

After he left and his notes were taken, he saw his next patient and knew that she could be the sister of the Anderson boy. She was just as much trouble, but in a different way. She was hurt in a scuffle outside the playground where she went to school. No one knew what had happened to her other than her bumps and bruises. Whatever had happened, she wasn't telling anyone. Instead, she took it out on those around her. Which meant him today. He finally had enough of her talking to him like he wasn't an adult and stepped back from examining her nose, which had been broken in whatever had happened.

"Listen here. I didn't hurt you, so you stop talking to me like I'm your worst enemy. All I'm trying to do is to patch you up so that you don't die of an infection or worse." She said it was none of his business what had happened. "I didn't ask you what happened. So keep your teeth behind your lips before someone takes exception to your words and hits you again."

She stared at him, so shocked that he could only stand there and think about what he'd said. Someone had hit her. And if he didn't miss his bet, he'd put money on someone of authority over her, like perhaps a teacher or a parent. He quietly asked her who had hit her.

"She said I'd go to prison if I told." Her voice was just as low as his had been, and when she looked around, he did as well. "I'm not a bad kid. I just have all this energy that makes me seem like one, but I do all my homework and get it all right. She said that I was surly and mean. I don't even know what surly means."

"It means you're bad-tempered and unfriendly. You're not that at all." Though ten minutes ago, he might have thought she was. "How long has she been beating on you?"

"Since I got in her class." Since school wasn't in session, he had to figure that she was doing this all summer long. Not to mention throughout the previous school year. No wonder she was unfriendly and surly. "You're not going to tell on me, are you? I don't want to go to prison where my mom is. That place is terrible."

"I would have to know who did it to you. You didn't tell me. Also, you wouldn't go to prison at all for a teacher to be beating the snot out of you when you've no reason to be around her." He eyed her. "You don't go seeking her out, do you? I mean, you just stay away from her all the time, I'm guessing."

"She finds me when I'm not looking. Then she makes me get in her car and takes me to her home. After she beats me up, she makes me dust her house and run the sweeper. It hurts after she beats me up, but

I still have to pull my weight." He might not know for sure who it was, but it was being narrowed down with each part of the story he got. He'd bet anything that it was Mrs. Jacobson. The elderly teacher who taught seventh grade. She was known to hire kids to do her housework, then not pay them. It seemed to him that she had found herself a better way to keep house. Beating the kids that came around. "Are you going to tell on me? She said that she'd make it so that it looked like I was robbing her and she was knocking me around to keep me from taking all her stuff. She doesn't have anything that I want in her nasty old house."

"Do you trust me, Shelly?" She told him that she didn't trust adults. "I know what you mean. If Mrs. Jacobson was doing that to me, I'd not trust them either."

"How did you know?" He said he was a good guesser. "You're the first one to have guessed right. Some of the police told me that they knew it was some boy that I didn't want to go out with. I'm only thirteen years old. I don't need a boyfriend. All the boys at my school are nerds anyway."

"You'll change your mind someday. But if you trust me, I think we can get this all cleared up in no time. I want to call the police." She backed away from him like he was going to hit her. "Did I say I was going to? No, all I said was I want to call them. They'll be able to make sure that she doesn't hurt any more kids, too. I think she might be doing this to a couple more kids that she knows as well."

"She is. Marly and Denise have been beaten up, too. She likes to use a sock full of apples on us." He wondered if there were more bruises on her body than he'd been allowed to see, but didn't push it. "I don't want to go to the police, Doc. If I do, then I'll go to prison for sure."

"I can promise you on my mother's heart that you will not go to prison for telling on her. She's a mean bully and deserves what she gets." Shelly told him that was a good promise. "It's the best one that I know. You don't deserve to be treated this way, and it's all on her, not on you. She'll be the one going to jail. And for a long time, if I have anything to say about it."

She sat there for several minutes staring at him before she spoke again. "I like your momma. She's one of the best people around. If I tell her that you lied to me, what will she do to you?"

"It will break her heart, and that would break mine as well. But nothing is going to happen to you. If you can get Marly and the other girl, Denise, to work with the police as well, she'll be going to jail tonight." She didn't ask if he promised this time, but nodded her head slowly. "I will protect you like I would my wife."

"All right, but I'm going to tell your momma

if you have lied to me. She'll be so upset with...Doc,
I hurt all over my body when I go there. I think she
enjoys hurting me. And when she tells me I'm going
to prison, she laughs like it's a done deal, and that's
where I'm going to end up. I don't want to go there."
He said that she wouldn't, and he had his nurse call the
police. But to come in the back door so no one would
be the wiser. "Yeah, she might be watching me. It's
about time for me to go back to her house. She usually
finds me about Thursday. I can sometimes hide away
until Friday, but she's good at catching me."

She keeps tabs on the girls that she has in her
house, he'd bet anything. As soon as Officer Pauly
walked into the little office, he knew things were going
to be all right. Pauly had three kids about the same age
as Shelly, and he'd bet anything he knew how to talk
to little girls to get information from them. As soon as
he left them to their business, he had to sit down in his
office and breathe. If his mom found out that he'd lied
to the young girl, she'd be so disappointed in him that
his own heart would break. Then it would break when
Debra told him how disappointed in him she was as
well.

When Pauly came to find him, he was just
finishing up with another patient. As soon as he saw
his face, he had a feeling that Shelly had told him
everything. Even more than she'd told him. After

going to his office with the older man, he was asked to sit down. His heart was in his throat when he found out just how badly the young girls were being beaten.

"She uses a sock with apples and quarter rolls in it to beat them with it. Shelly showed me her back, and I'd kill someone who did that to my kid. And this ain't no boy that she's been avoiding either. This is a grown assed woman knocking around a bunch of kids on account of her being their teacher. I'm going to go and arrest her even as we speak here, and you can bet that she's not going to be getting out of jail anytime soon. Judge Merkel will have her behind bars for months. His little girl killed herself when she was being bullied by a teacher, and he's vowed to keep them out of the system so that they can't hurt anyone else's little girls."

"I'll send her to the hospital now. So with a thorough exam, you'll have evidence for this." He said he was going to talk to the other girls as well. "Send them here, and I'll make sure you have all the evidence you need. I promised her that she'd not go to jail. You didn't suggest that she did, did you?"

"No. Why would you think she'd need to hear that?" He told him of the things that Jacobson was telling the girls. "She did mention that she didn't want to go to prison, but I didn't think about why she'd say that. No, I didn't suggest she go to jail. She's not the bully in this, but the victim. No, she'll be all right once we have Jacobson in jail. I'm betting there are a lot of kids who are being used by that woman. I heard rumors about her when I was a kid in middle school. You think she's been doing this so long that I'd remember her? Christ, that's just terrible that no one came forward before this. You did a good thing there, Kahana. Thanks for your help in getting this taken care of."

"I was just doing my job in keeping her safe." He nodded and left with Shelly. He was going to run her to the hospital in town to make sure that she had a good examination. Kahana had to be worried about how much he'd not been able to see because she fought him. And he wondered for all the little girls in town when they might have been a part of her housecleaning crew.

~*~

Reading over the form three times, Debra was satisfied that everything was spelled right and that everything else was in order. She hated to get paperwork back from someone, and there were misspelled words and loopholes bigger than her head. She liked clean paperwork that said what it was supposed to say and not get all mixed up with having to try to figure out what the hell it was talking about.

Lying the paperwork to the side, she started on the next form that she had to read over. She didn't mind this kind of work. It made her feel good when a contract went out as perfectly as she could make it. When there was a knock at her door, she looked up and smiled at Axel. He had his hands full of files.

"I'm running to the courthouse to file these. Also, to the notary to have things notarized for tomorrow's summons. Did you need anything while I'm out? I was going to grab lunch for the two of us." She said that she would have things to go to the courthouse in the morning, but nothing today. "Good. I have to say, it's nice having an extra person around. I never realized how little I was getting done until you showed up."

"How did I have anything to do with your workload?" He laughed and said that he was keeping up with her. "Oh well, I've not been working very long this week, and I had a lot to catch up on. Did you hear that the partners are ready to buy? I'll be so happy to have that taken care of."

"I bet you will. Well, I'm off. I'll be back in about an hour, depending on how busy the courthouse is when I get there." He turned away, then back. "By the way, my service is on, so you don't have to worry about catching my phone. I don't know why I don't use it more often. It's sometimes a godsend to have it around."

After he left, she got back to work. She had missed a great deal in not working for a month and was glad that she was getting things taken care of. Not only did she have the ten cases that her grandda had left for her, but there were the things that she was taking care of for the family as well, especially for Millie and Charlie.

Her mom was still in jail and looked to be in there for a while now. The judge wouldn't be coming through for another two weeks, and that was plenty of time to get a case filed against her for trying to kidnap her grandchildren. There were other charges pending as well, but that was the one that was going to get her the most jail time. That and breaking poor Charles' arm like she did. The kid was milking it too, she thought with a smile.

After getting the forms taken care of and read over, she worked on the rest of the things she had on her desk. There were the things that her grandda had left in addition to things that needed her attention about the money she'd inherited. And that in and of itself was a lot of headache.

Billions of dollars were hers to do with what she wanted. She had houses that she could visit, as well as whole plots of land that were just sitting and ready for her to do something with them. That was going to be the hardest, she thought. Trying to figure out what she was to do with five thousand acres of land out west. Or the two hundred that were along the eastern border.

There were things that she'd not looked too deeply into because she'd been so busy. There were jewels that were hers to wear as well. Mines of not just diamonds but also other gems and gold as well. Taking a deep breath, she started to feel overwhelmed again and had to lean back in her chair and breathe deeply.

She wasn't as worried about having another heart attack as she had been. It would still catch her off guard that, for as young as she was, she'd had one. Lucky for her, there had been people around her who knew what to do when she was having it, or there would be no telling how she would have survived, if at all. Debra was taking care of herself and eating right. She took her medications when she was supposed to and put her feet up when that was necessary as well. There was no way she was going to have another one if she could be doing something about it. As she was feeling less overwhelmed again, Axel came into her office.

"I got you the veggie sub without mayo. I thought that was the one you liked." She said it was and was glad that it was made with whole wheat bread instead of white. Taking a bite of it, she could taste all the freshness in it and moaned. "I have a turkey sub without mayo. I'm cutting back as well. You might be good for me to have around if you keep eating healthy like this."

"That's what Kahana said about eating at home. He wanted steak last night, but since I have to eat it in moderation, I wanted salmon. He ended up eating the salmon with me and said he didn't feel as bloated afterwards. He's not what I'd call a romantic sometimes." They both laughed at her joke. "I noticed, too, that you go running with him in the morning. I'd like to go, but I'm not up to the speed that he is yet. I don't want him to have to change his routine just because I can only go about two miles so far. He goes ten. That's quite a workout for me."

"I love running in the morning. Everything is fresh. Plus, I get to hang out with my brother, so that makes it doubly nice." She took another bite of her sandwich and grinned at Axel when he ate part of his sub. She enjoyed sharing lunch with her brother-in-law. He was funny and just nice to be around. "Mac has a doctor's appointment in the morning. I did tell you that I was going to be late, correct?"

"You did. But you said you'd have your service on, so I'm not to worry about your calls." He nodded that was right. "How are things going with her doctor visits? I know she's only going once a month right now. You two must be excited to be having a baby."

"Excitement is an understatement. And I love going to the doctor with her. I want to be at every one. I've even moved my courthouse appearances around her appointments. I don't know how much longer I'm going to be able to do that, but I can do it now, and that's what matters. Next month, she gets another scan to make sure that the baby is growing the way that he should." She asked him if it was a boy. "I don't know. I just call it a him sometimes or a her the other. I don't want to call him and it. That just sounds like I don't care when I do."

"Well, I'm having fun watching the two of you. As he told you, we're not using any kind of birth control, so when it happens, it happens for us. You'll have to be able to tell us what you think of your doctor. All the stuff you're going through right now, I want to know so that I can be prepared for it when our time comes."

After lunch, she went back to work on her cases and followed up on the things that she had on her list. She'd always been good at having a list for things. She thought that was why she was able to get so much done in a day that she followed her list every day. She wasn't good at taking one to the grocery store and usually regretted it when she got home. She would spend all kinds of money and forget what she went in there for in the first place. Kahana was good at making a list for the store. He usually had things like measurements, too, when he had to go to the hardware store. Which was why she had three containers of cocoa, and he had no extra wood lying around.

At five o'clock, she was ready for home. They'd been cooking out a lot lately, and she was looking forward to grilled chicken with a nice salad. So far, she'd not been cheating that much on her diet. She stopped eating chips and dips. There were no more cookies in the house, and she was having a good time reading the labels with Kahana's help. She'd found out just by accident that just because it said low sodium on the label, it might still have a lot of it in the vegetables. That's what reading the labels had gotten her. A good understanding of what was on the can versus the ingredients on the can.

Walking home took her about an hour. It wasn't really that far, but she would meet people along the way, and she'd get distracted. Even when there weren't people around, she'd be distracted. Yesterday, for about fifteen minutes, she watched the construction crew take down a house that should have been taken down years ago.

It was mind-blogging to her to see how they did it. Like they had a plan. She was sure that they did, but she wouldn't have been able to do it. She'd have the entire block down using the big de-construction machine, what she decided to call it from now on.

When she got home, she changed her clothing to go out in the yard and mess with the flowers. They pretty much came up on their own and bloomed beautifully, but today she was going to pick some of them to have on their table when they ate. There were such wonderful colors that she could hardly pick the ones that she saw. She was still having fun when Kahana pulled into the driveway after he got home from work.

"You look very summery. Those shorts are beautiful." He laughed at her when she tried to pull them down to a good length. "I was just kidding you. You do look like you're having fun, however."

"I am. I thought I'd bring some of the colors in the house tonight." He helped her with her bouquet, careful of his suit. She loved him so much that she had to pause sometimes when she thought about him loving her. "We're having grilled chicken tonight, and April was able to find us some corn on the cob that wasn't too expensive."

"Sounds delicious. I found some of that low-dairy ice cream that you can have. I thought we'd have a dish of it after dinner. I'm all for trying it. If I don't like it, I have regular ice cream that I can have. You have to eat the good for you stuff." She didn't mind and told him as much. "The lady at the store said it was supposed to taste like ice cream, but she didn't know. I took her word for it that you might not care for it. I don't know. I read the ingredients. I think it's just fluffed up more than normal ice cream is."

"I'll try it to see what it tastes like. You know me, I'm willing to try anything once." He kissed her when she got out of the flower garden. "Your brother and I are working out well. Today we had lunch together, and when he left tonight, he reminded me a hundred times that he was going to be late in the morning. He has a doctor's appointment with Mac."

"I'm glad he goes to her appointments with her. I know that I'm going to go to yours with you." She asked him why he wasn't going to be delivering their babies. "I'd be a wreck if I had to do that. I'm better off behind you than I would be in front of you during that time. I don't even want to be his or her pediatrician. They'll be better off if I don't do anything like that at all."

"All right. I guess I can see that. I wouldn't want to be our attorney even if it were allowed. I would be so sick with worry that I'd mess things up that I'd probably have another heart attack." He kissed her again, and she told him she loved him. "Did you have a good day at work?"

"I did. I'm glad that you and Axel are getting along so well. I'm doing well with the two nurses that I have now. And I love you as well." Entering the house, they put the flowers in a vase, and Kahana went up to change. Following him to do the same, she wondered how she'd lived this long without him in her life. He was her everything.

Chapter 10

Penrod was finding all kinds of things about Mrs. Jacobson that kind of made him a little ill. She'd not only been using the girls in her class to clean her house after beating them up, but she'd also been having her lawn mowed by the boys for better grades. And most of the time, when they were mowing her lawn, she made them pay for gasoline and didn't give them anything to drink. She had a big yard, too.

"Are you sure you don't mind looking into the Jacobson stuff? I know you're homicide, but right now we don't have anything going on." He told his boss that he didn't mind at all that he liked to stay busy. "Good. Are you finding out anything that can be used to bring her in? I remember her from when I was in school. I would have thought that she would have retired by now. I guess if she's doing her job, they don't care what else she might be up to."

"She's been doing this for years. I remember the rumors from when I was in seventh grade. I was never any trouble, so she had no reason to pick me out but I had heard there were kids who were being singled out for lawn work." He asked him why he didn't look into it. "I was just glad that I didn't have to mow her lawn too. My dad made us take turns mowing the lawn all summer. We had a riding mower, but all the trimming had to be done by a push mower. I was a lazy kid like everyone else was back then."

"My sister said she knows of a couple of girls who had to do her housework. Bennie wasn't a part of it, but she remembered these two girls from her class who had to stay over until the housework was finished up. I wonder why no one reported her. Or do you think anyone would have listened to a bunch of kids?" He told him that they'd probably not have listened to anyone back then. And nowadays, with the threat of prison being hung over their heads, it would be a lot harder to get them to come forward. "I'm just glad that she was able to talk to an officer who had a little knowledge about what was going on. I guess she was beaten up pretty badly around her back and ribs."

"I saw the report. I guess we'll have to run her in for abuse. Or would you call it bullying? Either way, she's going to be facing some jail time and probably lose her job." He said he hoped she lost her job. "I am as well. To think this has been going on for decades, and no one ever said a word about it. I'd do well in her class, even I'd heard the rumors. Just so I'd not get the shit beaten out of me."

"I hear you." Working on what he could about

the case, he was worried that some of the parents were going to be pissed off because it had been going on for so long. Without the help of Shelly, there is no telling how much longer it would have been happening. As it was now, they were asking people around his age if they'd been a part of the crew that went to her house to clean or mow. That to him was just sad.

After putting away the file when he'd done all he could for the day, he pulled open one of the cold cases that had been on his desk for a few months. It's not as if he didn't look at it sometimes, but it was so old he was having trouble finding people who even cared about it. There had been a murder back in thirty-nine that killed two people and injured twenty-three others.

The murderer had been a man and his wife, who had been serving breakfast at the local — back then it had been a local restaurant — place that had served whoever came in with money. A lot of people around town took exception to that, saying that it was a sin for them to serve anyone who wasn't white. The couple that ran the place had been killed one morning while they were serving breakfast, and the entire place had been shot up too while customers had been eating. It was such a mess that it took them days to figure out that the man and woman who had been killed were the owners of the place. They just lumped them into the group of eaters and wondered where the couple was.

Making notes on the page where the report had been filed, he read how the man had been shot in the head at close range, and the woman had been brutally murdered. It didn't say how she'd been murdered, and since there was no autopsy done, he had no way of knowing how either of them had died. Had they been beaten? Was she raped as well as killed? There was no way of telling after all this time, as most of the people who had been in there that morning had all died or had long since forgotten about it ever happening.

He'd had a lead of someone being there as a child, but all he could remember was his mom shoving him under the table until it was over, then carrying him out so that he'd not see all the blood.

"I tell you what. That place was so full of holes that you could have gotten a breeze wherever you sat." He asked him if he had ever heard who had done it. "Oh no, not me. I was just a kid. There had been rumors that the church had done it, and that's why only the two people who were killed were done the way that they were."

"How did the old man die? It was said that he was shot in the head at close range." He said he'd never heard that part of it, but he knew that the old woman had suffered. "How? Did you ever figure that out? All it says in the file is that she was murdered, but nothing about it. There were no pictures of her either. But there was of the man."

"Don't know. There were some rumors like I told you, that the church did it to them. They didn't like that she'd serve the blacks like she did the white folks. I don't think she ever saw color when she was serving up her food. She was just a nice old lady who happened to like to cook for people. The old man, he'd run the register. My mom told my dad once that he gave away more than people paid for back then. I don't know any more than that. I remember it, like it was yesterday, but as far as details about what went on. I didn't see anything other than the backside of the table I was hiding under."

He had a feeling that this was going to be one of those unsolvable cases. Anyone who might have had a grudge against the people had long since died. There were no witnesses who were around anymore for the same reason. And the one source that he had turned out to have been a six-year-old kid that had the sense to stay where his momma had shoved him so he'd not get shot at too. When he'd gotten back to the office, he put it aside as he had with the other two files. They were too old to be solved now, and he had a feeling that that was why they were on his desk; no one knew how to solve them.

At the end of his shift, he turned in all the paperwork he'd found on Jacobson. They were going to arrest her in the morning for bullying kids. He didn't know how much time she'd get with it, but he knew that there were people around who didn't much care for the older woman. She'd been teaching classes at the middle school longer than he'd been around and was glad that he'd never been in trouble with her. Like he'd told his captain, he had enough mowing going on without having to mow someone else's yard for the heck of it.

Penrod hated his place. He'd been living there since he'd gotten out of the academy. It was a condo like his other brothers had had, and he couldn't stand to live with neighbors close by all the time. Not to mention the kids who would use his part of the yard as a play yard. He didn't mind so much them using it, but when he was on night shift, and they played right outside his windows, it made him have difficulty falling asleep and staying that way. He wanted his own home and yard so that he could own something more than a condo and not have much to show for it. He also wanted to mow his own grass. He'd not tell anyone that, but he did want to smell the first season's grass being mowed. Then after that, he'd hire someone to do it. He also wanted to plant a nice little vegetable patch so that he could grow his own tomatoes. His favorite snack.

He'd been looking, but he'd admit that he'd not

been looking very hard. He loved both of his brothers' homes and the way they were set back off the road so they'd not be in traffic a great deal. He also liked the fact that there were flowers around their homes that they took care of. That was what he wanted, a yard that he could have some fun in, like they seemed to be doing.

Having his mom and dad over for dinner sometimes was something that he wanted as well. He loved having a meal with them and was glad that they lived close enough that he could. While they were busy with other things in their lives, they never turned down an opportunity to have a meal with one of their kids. He was going to do the same thing when he had a family. Always have time for his loved ones. He was just getting ready to have a bowl of cereal when his cell phone rang. It was his brother, Stamos. He thought that of all his brothers, he was closest to him.

"I've been running that article about the *Little Dew Drop* restaurant like you asked. So far, all I've gotten is people not remembering it being there. There was some talk about the shooting, but nothing you can use. They'd heard from a friend of a friend of a friend about it, and they didn't have much in the way of details. Did you talk to that man in the nursing home? What was his name?" He told him. "That's right, Tommy Hill. He's the only child that I can find who was there that morning. I'm still looking, but I'm thinking that you have a dead case for yourself. What have you been able to find out?"

"As much as you had. Tommy told me how he'd been shoved under the table and didn't get out until his mom took him out of the place. He couldn't even remember if his parents had been shot or not. I'm assuming that they were, but it must not have been all that serious." Stamos told him that most of the others who were shot had superficial wounds. "That's what makes it so weird that the couple that were shot were murdered. They were singled out, obviously, but why? Other than the fact that they were servicing whoever came in, there isn't a thing to indicate that they were doing anything wrong. Would the church really have done this to them, you think?"

"Back then, who knows. Nowadays, you'd have so much information on the shooting that it would take a couple of files to hold it all. Not to mention lawsuits against the place for not having any kind of provisions in place to keep guns out." He agreed with him. "I only called to see if you'd gone to see Tommy. I'm sorry that it didn't pan out the way that you hoped. But I didn't expect too much as he'd only been about five when it happened. It might have been something that he would have remembered, but it's doubtful after all this time he'd have much in the way of details."

He was glad that his brother gently bullied him into having dinner with him. He didn't want to have cold cereal again tonight when he could have a nice cheeseburger and fries. He was suddenly starving for a good meal and was glad that he'd be able to have it with his best buddy. Stamos was a good man, and he loved to hang out with him.

Getting ready to go, he was glad that he was going to pick him up. He didn't mind driving himself, but sometimes it was fun to be carted around. When Stamos picked him up, they talked about the other files on his desk as well as the upcoming trial of Jacobson. He hoped that she got a lot of jail time for hurting such a good kid.

"I agree. She's had this coming for a while now. I think that when I was in her class, she didn't much care for me, but since I was getting good grades, there was no reason to 'tutor' me. I'm sure that I would have told Mom and Dad about it had I been a victim of hers. They would have done something about her then." He told his brother that he'd heard the rumors as well, but never put much stock in it, as the kids were usually goof-offs as well as getting terrible grades. "That's more than likely why she chose them. They wouldn't have been believed over her and that was what she was counting on."

"You think? That makes sense. I never thought

of it like that." He said he usually thought of the worst-case scenario when it came to writing a story. "I would imagine. You'd have to have a very open mind about things as well."

"I do." They finished their meal and had a nice visit. On his way home, he talked about how he was going to turn the file over to the boss and tell him there wasn't anything he could do about it. There had just been too much time that had passed since it had happened. "I'll see what I can find out about the newspaper articles that might have been run then. I'll give you a call if I find anything."

After saying good night, they parted ways and knew that tomorrow they'd be talking again. It was nice to have a good friend as a brother, and he was going to make sure that he told him that every day. He loved all his family, but got along best with Stamos.

~*~

Kahana was finished for the day at six-thirty. It was a little later than he would normally be in the office, but it had been a good day. No one was hurt today, and there had only been a couple of people that he'd had to send to the hospital for more tests. He could do a lot of things in his office, but x-rays weren't one of them.

The two of them had been walking around town after dinner. The first night they'd done it, they had stopped for ice cream, but had since stopped doing that. It was bad for Debra, and he didn't need the extra calories either. So they met people on their walks and got to know the town better that he'd grown up in. The people started looking for them when they went down the main street in their town.

"I've been thinking about my office at home. I'm going to make sure that I don't spend all evening in there unless I have a large case. I don't want to miss out on time with you when I'm holed up in the office." He said he loved that plan. "You just want to be able to get laid more often. Though I don't know how that would work since we make love twice a day as it is. You're wearing me out."

"I'm glad you said that because I've been thinking the same thing. I sleep like the dead when I go to bed, but it's not enough. I'm worn to death, and I don't think that I've ever been more in love with you than I am right now. I'm betting that tomorrow I'll love you even more." She thanked him, and they held hands. "Tomorrow I have to go to the hospital to take some tests of my own. I had a mole removed a few months ago, and they want to make sure that it's healing well and that I don't have any trouble with it. It wasn't cancer, but I've learned to take better care of watching my body for things that I didn't before."

"I'm glad to hear that. I didn't know about the mole. I'm glad that you got it tested." He said that he was as well because it worried him a great deal. "Then I'm doubly glad that you got it tested. You must have worried your family when you did that."

"I messed up with that. I didn't tell anyone that I was having the test done until it was over. The doctor pointed out that they'd not trust me with not telling them something so important again if I didn't come clean. He was right, they were hurt about it, so I've learned a valuable lesson in that. I'm going to make sure I keep up with my body and tell my family when I have something that worries me." She asked him if he'd been able to find anything else on his body. "No. Thank goodness. I had a patient who had a mole that they let go, and it turned out to be cancerous. It has spread to her lymph nodes, and she had to have chemotherapy to combat the illness. She's doing much better now, but it had been scary back then for the two of us."

"I'm glad she's doing better and that you are too. I don't know what I'd do without you in my life." He said that he felt the same way about her. "Good. Then we make sure that we never lie to each other ever. Omission is as much a lie as the actual lie. Let's make sure we never do that to each other."

"I agree." They were nearly home when they were stopped by some of the neighborhood kids. They were wondering if there was going to be a tournament this year for the best-decorated house. "You'll have to talk to Gilman. He's the one who is in charge of that part of the family. I know that he's working late tonight, but he should be around tomorrow if you want to hit him up for an answer."

"We'll do that. Last year he had the best house display." He was the only younger brother with a house, too. And since he was an electrical engineer, it stood to reason he'd have the best house.

However, he never participated in the contest. He only gave out the prize of five hundred dollars for the best house. It wasn't really all that much when you thought of all the work that went into doing it every year, but it was fun, and people really got into decorating their homes for the holidays.

"It's still so far away until Christmas. Do they really start decorating their homes already? That seems like a lot of work if they're doing it now." He said that he'd bet that Gilman already had his display all mapped out and ready to be put up. "I guess I have a lot to learn about this family. Have any of you ever won?"

"No. And it's probably a good thing too. The people in town really love it, and we have long car lines of people coming from all over just to see the displays. It's really a big thing." She said she was getting excited, too. "I've never decorated before being in a condo, so I'm looking forward to having a house that I can go all out in. We don't participate either, but it's fun watching things go up around town. Even the storefronts get in on it."

By the time they were home, they'd walked three miles. It was a good walk too, and since the weather had cooled off during the evening hours, it was quite pleasant to walk. During the hottest part of the evening, they wouldn't walk so far, but they did tonight.

"I've got some paperwork to work on in the morning, so I have to leave first thing." Kahana said he had rounds in the morning, so he had planned to leave earlier, too. "Good. That way, I don't have to get out of a warm bed with you still in it. I hate that more than you know. You look so warm and cozy that I simply want to go back to bed with you and forget the day."

"I know that feeling. When I get called out in the middle of the night, I feel the same way. Being a doctor had never been so hard before you came along in my life." They decided to watch some television before heading to bed. They didn't watch any shows that they had to watch, but they did enjoy the occasional show when they turned it on. For all the channels they had, they didn't watch all that much. "I have to get to bed. I'm exhausted tonight. Dinner was good, and I'm still full from it."

"I know what you mean. I feel the same way, but not a stuffed kind of full. Just full because I ate well. I think that made more sense in my head." He told her that he understood what she meant. "Good. I can always depend on you to know what I'm trying to say. It's so nice to have you around all the time."

As they headed up to bed, his cell phone rang. It was the hospital, and since he wasn't on call, he told the service to call the doctor on duty. She told him how she had tried, but he wasn't answering, and it was an emergency. Pissed off a little, Kahana got dressed again and made his way in to see what was going on. If it were a delivery, he was going to be all right with that, but nothing else. When you're on call, you'd better answer the phone, damn it.

"Doctor Hathaway, I'm sorry that you had to be bothered, but we tried to call the doctor on duty several times without any luck. I know we have the right number as we've had to call it before." He didn't take it out on the staff and told them that he was all right. "Mrs. Sheppard came in with chest pains. We've run an EKG on her, and it doesn't show anything. But she wanted a doctor to tell her that instead of us nursing staff."

"I'll take care of it." He went into the cubicle and saw that the woman was hooked up to the monitors and was doing fine. She was eating a cheeseburger while sitting in the bed. He asked her how she was feeling. "You look good. I'm to understand that the nurses said that your monitor showed that you're not having a heart attack. However, if that's the way you eat all the time, it's no small wonder that you have chest pains. It might be just heartburn you're having."

"I want tests done that show that I'm all right." He told her that he'd do that, but her insurance might not pay for extensive testing since nothing was showing up so far. "I don't care. I'd rather be safe than sorry. You run the tests and let me decide if I'm having heart trouble or not."

"I can do that. First of all, you'll have to wait a few hours because you've something on your stomach right now." That wasn't true, but he'd been told that she does this sort of thing all the time when there was nothing wrong. He'd heard that she was lonely and that was why she'd make her way into the emergency room about three times a month. "I can run blood tests on you to see what I can find in the meantime."

"All right. You do it all." He would, too, just to make his point. He'd taken care of this particular woman before and knew that she could be a pain in the ass if he didn't find anything wrong with her. "If my insurance doesn't pay it, I'll have words with them, too. I don't like this feeling of having chest pains."

"As I said, I'll run what I can right now and

see what we can find. Your EKG or electrocardiogram shows me, and we'll go from there. So far, it looks good, too." She asked him why she was having such pains then. "I don't know, but I can look into what I can find. As I said, it might be a really bad case of heartburn or GERDS. Gastroesophageal reflux disease can feel pretty bad, I've been told."

"You run the tests, and I'll deal with it until then. Unless you can give me a little something to tide me over. I hurt like the dickens." He said that he'd give her something small for the pain, but it couldn't be too much since he was going to be running tests on her. "I understand. You just give me what you can, and I'll feel better for it."

"Do you have your gallbladder?" She told him that she did, and no one had asked her that before. "Never? Well, we can run some tests to see if that's it. I'm not saying that it is, but we can have a look to see if it's inflamed or not. If it's bad enough, and again, I'm not saying it is, we'll be able to remove it, and that will solve your issues. They can do the surgery in the morning, and you'll be better than you have in a long time."

"Then I hope that's it. I would like to feel better than I have in a good long while." He went out of her room and stopped at the nurses' station. After ordering some labs and a C-scan of her belly, he made sure that she had something for pain. He wouldn't give her much; she was a little bitty thing, but he'd make sure that she wasn't in too much pain when they did the tests on her.

At a quarter to midnight, he knew that she was going to have to have her gallbladder removed. It was quite inflamed and tender to the touch. Setting up her surgery time made him feel good that he'd been able to find it. Mrs. Sheppard was happy as well. Now she could get on with living her life, she told him without pain. He hoped that this would do the trick. He felt sorry for the older woman.

After talking to her again about the surgery and how it was going to be performed, he made his way to the doctors' lounge. He was going to catch a few winks before morning when the surgery was going to happen. He'd be there when she came out, but her care would be that of the surgeons. He was never so happy to hand over a patient as he was this one. She was nice and everything, but she'd been looked over too much. He was hoping that she'd find that she felt so good that she'd not have to come to the hospital again.

On his way home at nine in the morning, he decided to stop and get some bagels. Debra could have one that was sugar-free, so he got two of them to join her. As soon as he was home, he remembered that she had things to do this morning and had left before he got home.

Disappointed, he ate his bagel in the kitchen and wished that he had a less constraining job than being a doctor. Then he remembered the look on Mrs. Sheppards face when she left for surgery, and he decided he had the best job of all. He was a good doctor, he told himself, and would continue to be from now on.

Before You Go...

HELP AN AUTHOR

write a review

THANK YOU!

Share your voice and help guide other readers to these wonderful books. Even if it's only a line or two, your reviews help readers discover the author's books so they can continue creating stories that you'll love. Log in to your favorite retailer and leave a review. Thank you.

AWARD WINNING, BESTSELLING AUTHOR

Kathi S. Barton is an award-winning and bestselling author known for her steamy paranormal romances and unforgettable characters. A recipient of the prestigious Pinnacle Book Achievement Award, her books have topped the charts on Amazon and All Romance eBooks, earning her a loyal global readership.

Kathi lives in Nashport, Ohio, with her husband, Paul. When she's not crafting passionate love stories set in magical worlds, she enjoys camping, exploring local auctions, and attending county fairs, where Paul showcases his artwork and pottery. Her creative spark—fueled by a muse she describes as a cross between Jimmy Stewart and Hugh Jackman—brings her stories to vivid, heartfelt life.

Paranormal romance with plenty of heat is her favorite genre, and she loves connecting with her readers. Feel free to reach out—Kathi would love to hear from you.

Email: aaronskiss@gmail.com

Follow Kathi on her blog: http://kathisbartonauthor.blogspot.com/

www.ingramcontent.com/pod-product-compliance
Lightning Source LLC
Chambersburg PA
CBHW031959170626
46807CB00006B/2563